THE DETECTIONS OF DR. SAM: JOHNSON

THE GREAT DETECTIVES

LILLIAN DE LA TORRE

THE DETECTIONS OF DR. SAM: JOHNSON

Xanadu

British Library Cataloguing in Publication Data
The detections of Dr. Sam: Johnson
I. Title
823′.914 [F]
ISBN 0-85480-012-4

First published in the USA in 1984 by International Polygonics Ltd
This edition published 1989 by Xanadu Publications Ltd

Printed and bound in Great Britain by Cox & Wyman Ltd, Reading

To Mr. F.A.K.,

the onlie begetter of these insuing . . .

PROEM

To the Candid Reader

These mystery tales of an earlier day are not true. They are probable fictions, suggested by real personalities, places, and events of the Age of Johnson (1709–84), centering around the most towering figure of that age, Dr. Sam: Johnson himself, and narrated as if by his famous biographer, James Boswell. That none of her fictions will appear to outrage the inner truth of these great men or the age they lived in, is the earnest wish and belief of

THE AUTHOR

CONTENTS

1 The Tontine Curse 15

2 The Stroke of Thirteen 37

3 The Viotti Stradivarius 59

4 The Black Stone of Dr. Dee 85

5 The Frantick Rebel 107

6 Saint-Germain the Deathless 127

7 The Missing Shakespeare Manuscript 147

8 The Triple-Lock'd Room 171

THE TONTINE CURSE

(*London & Bath*, *1779*)

"There's a curse on the tontine," said the brewer's wife, and wept.

"Ma'am," replied Dr. Sam: Johnson positively, "there's a curse on every tontine."

Mr. Hosyer the portly brewer breathed hard through his jolly red nose. Mrs. Hosyer, buxom and motherly, buried hers in her kerchief and sobbed.

'Twas an unexpected prelude to what I had thought would be a purely legal confabulation. We sat in the dark-panelled inner room of Lloyd's Coffee-house, awaiting the others of the Hosyer tontine. At the head of the table, smiling to himself and saying nothing, sat the Hosyer lawyer, Theophilus Sedge, a pleasing little man, as rosy and round as a winter apple.

Seated next him, to support his legal opinion with my own, behold myself, James Boswell of Auchinleck, attorney and observer of mankind, being (I flatter myself) a not unpleasing personage with a swart complection, a long nose, and black hair tied back in the latest mode.

By the mantel-piece, staring sombrely into the glowing coals, stood my penetrating friend, Dr. Sam: Johnson. The fire-light fell on his heavy, deep-cut features, softening the old scars of the King's Evil. It glanced on his large bushy grizzle wig, and on the silver buckles of his square-toed shoes; it ruddied the plain brown stuff of his full-skirted coat; it glittered on his thoughtful light-grey eyes. Such was Dr. Sam: Johnson in the year 1779, being then seventy years of age.

Looking up at him across the table, I congratulated myself once more that I, though a Scot, and some thirty years his junior, had by my address and assiduity won the friendship and confidence of this extraordinary man. To the universal respect accorded him as the literary dictator of London, was added the admiration I felt for his less bruited exploits as a detector of crime and chicane. Over the years of our friendship, I had watched him, fascinated, as he detected the Flying Highwayman, the maker of the Wax-Work Cadaver, and many other practitioners of fraud and felony; and I had long since inly resolved one day to record for posterity, not only the life, but the *detections* of Dr. Sam: Johnson.

To this end 'twas ever my care to observe his proceedings, and still more, to be the cause of such further proceedings as might, by calling forth his powers, serve to enrich my record.

Such an occasion, I knew, must be offered by this curious affair of the Hosyer tontine; and accordingly, at my urging, hither he was come to make one at the counsel table. Now, in his manly, resonant, positive voice, he was making abundantly clear his adverse philosophy of the tontine.

"A curse on every tontine?" I repeated, willing to draw him out further. "How do you make that good?"

"Consider, Mr. Boswell." He took the chair nearest the fire, put his feet under the table, and squared himself to have his talk out. "Consider the very nature of a tontine. I say nothing to your Irish tontine; 'twill do as well, I suppose, as any other form of publick lottery. But permit me to characterize to you the vicious nature of a private tontine such as this one."

Lawyer Sedge, who had drawn up the Hosyer tontine in the first place, raised his frosty thistledown brows; but his smile was as bland as ever.

"To make such a tontine," pursued Johnson, "you gather together ten or a dozen infants of tender years—"

"Twenty," said the brewer.

"Twenty infants of tender years. For each infant let the parent stake, say, one thousand pounds—"

"Five thousand," said the brewer.

Dr. Johnson blew a soundless whistle through his pursed lips. "Whoo! You set the temptation high! Twenty infants at five thousand pounds—one hundred thousand pounds. Invest it in the funds—"

"My brother has the handling of it."

"Put it out at interest, and leave it there until nineteen of your twenty die. Then the whole sum becomes the property of the survivor. To the gouty, toothless, sapless, gustless twentieth old man falls a noble fortune, say eight hundred thousand pounds, if it be true as they say that money at interest doubles every twenty years."

"My brother has already doubled the fund."

"Bravo, Mr. Hosyer! In what business?"

"Ship insurance. My brother is one of the gentlemen yonder." The brewer nodded his head toward the outer room of the coffee-house, where the gentlemen of Lloyd's sat at the bare scrubbed tables and wrote insurance on the ships that ply out of London. Johnson looked at the lined faces, bent over their ciphering or frowning in close converse or just staring.

"A calling not without hazard," he remarked, "especially with the reverses of the American war. Well, well, let your brother's luck still hold, sixty or eighty years hence, some old gaffer, his relation, will be enriched with a princely fortune he'll never live long enough to enjoy. And the medium of his enrichment will be death, Mr. Boswell—death to his brothers and sisters, death to his cousins, his neighbours, his friends. Between each child and that fortune stand nineteen lives."

Mrs. Hosyer shuddered violently.

"And though no one of the twenty grow up so lost to virtue as to hasten his fortune by imbruing his hands in blood—yet consider what must be the effect of constantly wishing nineteen deaths? No, sir, there was never a private tontine but had a curse on it."

"If we but had back our ten thousand pounds!" cried Mrs. Hosyer. "It would stand between us and present ruin."

"No more o' that," cried Hosyer roughly. "The brewery will be very well."

"The tontine," said Lawyer Sedge smoothly, "was made Michaelmas four years ago, at the house of Mr. Breed Hosyer the ship-broker at Bath. He having made a second marriage, desired thus to provide for the sons of his first. The families of the tontine . . ."

I own I lost the thread. The families of the tontine had had ill luck, being swept by the small-pox, the colick, and the like.

"Alack!" said Dr. Johnson, "how many of these little creatures perish in their innocence! They are but lent to us. If we can raise one in three, we may call ourselves fortunate. Of twelve, Brewer Thrale has but four surviving."

"Of the tontine's twenty," said Hosyer grimly, "but four survive."

"But four!" cried Johnson aghast. "This is beyond the rule of nature! Who are the four?"

"My girl Sally, and Sister Macklin's Susan, and Mr. Sedge's boy, and my brother's heir."

"Pray, how has this come about?"

"The curse," muttered Mrs. Hosyer, and wrung her fingers.

"Sir," her husband began, "the children, them that lived through the small-pox, went on merrily enough, till a year gone we lost our eldest girl."

"By what means?"

The Hosyers spoke together. He said:

"An accident."

"She destroyed herself," said the wife. "She destroyed herself for love. Her marriage portion was lost—" some hidden bitterness burst forth, "and when the match she desired was broken, so was her heart; she hanged herself in her garters."

"I had reverses," muttered Hosyer pitifully.

"I wish we had never heard of the tontine! I wish we had our ten thousand pounds back!"

Hosyer looked baited. I thought how many times before he must have heard that whine. Sedge, still smiling, pulled forth a handsome repeater watch and looked from it to the outer door. A line between his frosty brows denied the smile.

Mrs. Hosyer sniffed back old grief and took up what was clearly an oft-rehearsed tale:

"We lost poor Annie in June. In July we went to Bath, to brother-in-law's. Brother-in-law lives like a nabob. His wife is the relict of a lord—if he has the brass, she knows how to spend it—and high though she holds her head, he's good to his own, and in the hot weather we were all there together."

Johnson: "All?"

Hosyer: "All—my wife and I, Sister Macklin, Lawyer Sedge, and brother-in-law and his new wife, and all the children. There was five in the schoolroom and the rest in the nursery—"

Mrs. Hosyer: "And in the stables Bob Hosyer, who at sixteen has set up for a rake on the nabob's money, and if my Lady don't ruin brother-in-law Hosyer, 'tis my belief Bob will."

Hosyer rebuked her with a look and went on in his heavy voice: "To be brief, sir, the schoolroom and the nursery had liberty to play in the grounds, and thence came the tragedy. They set sail on the millpond in a leaky old tub that foundered under them, and we were nigh to losing them all. My Sally, who is of intrepid mould, drew her cousin Susan to shore. Sedge's Clem was cadging sweetmeats in the buttery, and Bob Hosyer was lounging with the grooms. Sister Macklin thought it a mercy that she was dandling the littlest ones in the morning-room. But of that boatload of seven, five sank, and rose no more."

Mrs. Hosyer looked back on the tragedy:

"And we were like to lose Sally, for she lay like one dead till we nigh despaired of restoring her."

Hosyer: "'Twas that that saved her."

Johnson: "How mean you?"

Mrs. Hosyer: "While the pond was dragging, the children got some spoiled food, it being very hot summer weather. They was taken with the gripes and the flux, and fast did it carry 'em off. Sally and Susan had none, being put to bed with a posset; Bob Hosyer lived, for he dined with his elders; and as to Sedge's Clem, 'tis my belief that nothing can kill him."

Sedge acknowledged this compliment with a radiant beam.

"Fourteen children," concluded Mrs. Hosyer solemnly, "went down to Bath in July. Four came back. Is not this a curse?"

"Ma'am," says Johnson, "I devoutly hope so. Better a supernatural than a human agent."

"Be easy, ma'am," says Sedge soothingly. "I grieve with the bereaved, ma'am, in these horrid mishaps; but I see in them nothing more than the grief that flesh is heir to. As to the boat, ma'am, a leaking skiff will sink, and a child that cannot swim will sink with it; and as to the gripes and the flux, ma'am, 'tis my belief the little ones had somehow got at my Lady's white lead; for your sister-in-law's unnatural white, ma'am, to speak plainly, and past question 'tis paint, and will one day carry her off like the late lamented Countess of Coventry."

"Psst," hissed Hosyer, heralding by this undignified means the impressive entrance of Mr. Breed Hosyer and his consort, my Lady Rivers that was.

Mr. Breed Hosyer would have been impressive in any gathering. He wore the finest of sombre stuffs, set off at the throat with a fall of cobwebby lace; his buckles were set with brilliants, and he wore a priceless ring on his finger. His face was thin and worn in an agreeable way, as unlike his brewer brother as possible. He handed his lady to an armed chair with studied courtliness.

The nabob's wife was an edged beauty, thin and very fair. Her unnaturally white skin was carmined over her sharp cheek-bones. She wore an enormous head, and patches. She arranged her laced ruffles, and inclined the towering wig a fraction off the vertical to the company in general.

"Now, then," said Breed Hosyer in a sharp voice that smacked of the City, "what's to do here? Where's Sister Macklin? If I can fetch my Lady from St. James's, surely she can on with her pattens and step hither on time. No matter, brother, what's the cause of this meeting?"

Hiram Hosyer looked mighty put about at this abruptness, but he answered bluntly:

"To break the tontine and part the money among the children."

I was surprized enough; I had never heard of the breaking a tontine once regularly entered into. But two of our members fairly rose from their places in horror—the lawyer and the broker.

"Impossible!" they cried as one man.

"Do," says my Lady languidly, "break the tontine, Mr. Hosyer, and then you may make such a settlement upon my daughter as is right and proper for the child of the late Lord Rivers; for a dowerless female may hang herself these days, she can hope for no better fate."

"Unless she's the relict of a lord—" began Mrs. Hosyer angrily.

Breed Hosyer had recovered his suavity. Without paying the

least mind to the glowering females, he leaned forward and addressed his brother patiently:

"Look you, brother, 'tis beyond possibility. It strikes at the very basis of the tontine, if it may be abrogated at will. Sedge will bear me out."

The lawyer nodded.

"As to parting the money, the loss will be extream, the blow to my credit worse, if in the present precarious state of affairs I must suddenly realize the funds of the tontine. Pray what is the urgent reason for this unreasonable request?"

"The curse—the curse on the tontine—"

"Tschah," said Breed Hosyer in disgust. "Who has started up this old wives' tale? I'll not be a party to breaking the tontine for so foolish a reason. Be content, brother; Sally may one day have all, if—" he offered his wrist to his lady, and smiled back over his shoulder as they withdrew, "—if she lives so long."

Hiram Hosyer, purple, turned to Lawyer Sedge to expostulate; but the lawyer was looking at his watch, and in another minute he was gone.

We found ourselves in the footway before Lloyd's Coffee-house with the Hosyers. I was ready to be off; but Johnson lingered.

"Ma'am," says he, "this is a dire tale, and a powerful argument against leaky row-boats and summer victuals. But why, when it happened in July, is this a reason to break the tontine suddenly in November? What has happened since, to rouze your apprehensions?"

The Hosyers exchanged glances. The brewer bit his lip.

"Last night," said Mrs. Hosyer in a low voice, "we had like to lost Sally with the gripes and the flux."

"And it not being summer," said Hosyer, his eyes on his shoes, "and Sally being new-returned from a sojourn with my Lady her Aunt Hosyer—sir, I'm at my wits' end. I cannot afford to break with my brother. What shall I do?"

Johnson was frowning now.

"The gripes and the flux are no uncommon ail. We must proceed with caution. I must know more of the summer tragedies. Who set the children on to so perilous a voyage? Who supped in the nursery, and upon what dish? I must talk with Sally at once."

"Sir, 'tis impossible. Dr. Catnach gave us powders to make a draught to quiet her, and now she sleeps like the dead . . ."

The last words seemed to linger on the air. The buxom wife turned pale. Her eyes and her husband's met in a like apprehension, and by common consent they urgently beckoned a passing hackney-coach. Johnson mounted without demur, and I followed.

As the Jehu plied his whip, a dishevelled dame clacked up on hurried pattens. She stood on the footway gesticulating after us.

"Cicely Macklin," said Mrs. Hosyer; and for all her drawn face she laughed.

Sally was sleeping unharmed. We looked down upon her in the shadow of the tester. She was a beautiful child, budding to a seductive sixteen. I admired her peaches-and-snow complection, her perfect form beneath the counterpane. As we gazed the blue-veined lids fluttered and rose. Brilliant blue eyes scanned our faces, and for a flash a dimple shewed beside the pale, perfect lips.

Though not impervious to the appeal of femininity, Dr. Johnson dared not spare her. He questioned her gently.

"I found the boat launched," she whispered, "and when I could not disswade the children from embarking, I went along for the preventing of mischief."

Her eyes darkened; she closed them.

"I do not know who set them on."

"We must ask Susan Macklin, who alone of that unlucky boat-load survives," said I.

Nor did Sally know aught of that misfortunate supper in the nursery, for she and Susan, bedded, had had posset from the nurse's own hand.

"We must ask the nurse," said I.

"The nurse is dead," whispered Sally. "Save for Clem, every soul who ate at that table died."

"And what did you eat yesterday, my dear, at your Aunt Hosyer's?"

"What the rest ate."

"No comfits?"

"I had a comfit of fat little Clem Sedge—but he ate thrice as many."

"No bit of marrow-fat for yourself, no posset to sleep on?"

"No, sir, Bob gets the tid-bits at my uncle's. Stay, there was milk brought to my bed-side by the serving-wench."

"Well, my dear, be a good girl, and rest, and all will be well."

"Yes, sir."

The girl turned her face to the wall, and tears began to stream from her eyes.

"I'm afraid."

The brewer's wife smoothed the wide brow. The blue eyes closed.

"Ma'am," says Johnson, "I'll talk with Susan in the morning."

"'Tis Lord Mayor's Day," said Mrs. Hosyer. "Come the next day. Come to Mrs. Macklin's in the Poultry."

So the rendezvous was concerted.

The Lord Mayor's Show, and the humours of the mob, engrossed our interest on the morrow, and Sally Hosyer's no less, putting the rendezvous, for the nonce, from our minds.

Nevertheless we kept our rendezvous, and betimes. Dr. Johnson himself rouzed me at my lodgings. His face shocked me.

"We are summoned too late. Susan Macklin is dead, and Sally Hosyer despaired of."

We hastened down to the antient street called the Poultry. In the dark old house of the widow Macklin a dreadful sight met our eyes. Smothered under the bed's fallen tester lay Susan Macklin. When the tangle of cloth and wooden frame was pushed aside, I gazed with pity on a peaked little face and half-open skinny hands.

Cicely Macklin had no gestures left. She stood like a snow statue by her daughter's bed and spoke without expression.

"Many's the time I've warned her and Sally, and her brother that's dead in the mill-pond, many's the time I've bade them swarm up the appletree if they must play at sailors, and not up the canopy, for all my gear's old and rotten—"

Dr. Johnson regarded the heavy frame where it had splintered away. The edge of the crack dated from the days of the sailor-play, it was old and grey, but the rest was white and fresh, where it had parted and fallen in the night. Dr. Johnson regarded it with a grave face.

"Who lay in the house last night?"

Widow Macklin brought her remote eyes to fasten on him.

"Susan that's dead, and Sally that's dying, and Brother and Sister Hosyer, and I. We were all here for the Lord Mayor's Show, for this house commands it, and after it I gave them a bed, and Sally loves to share Susan's. 'Twas an ill hour for Sister Hosyer when she yielded to Sally's entreaties, scarce recovered as she was from her indisposition."

"Who knew of the plan?"

"Why, all here. Mr. Sedge said 'twas indulging the chits, but my Lady bade us humour the child for God's sake—"

"Mr. Sedge? My Lady? Were they here?"

"I said so. They were all here for the Lord Mayor's Show."

"Pray, ma'am, who was here?" Dr. Johnson asked.

"Mr. Sedge and Clem—Mr. Breed Hosyer and my Lady and Bob—Brother Hiram Hosyer and his wife and daughter—I and Susan; no one else, for the wench was off making holiday."

Her gaze slid away again; she straightened a lock on her daughter's ice-cold brow.

"Sally?"

"Sally?—Sally. Sally lies in my bed."

She gestured down the passage, and we left her.

Sally Hosyer lay in such another canopied bed in such another dark chamber, as still and as white as her cousin; but a shallow thread of pulse gave hope of her recovery. Her mother was chafing her cold hands, her father setting hot bricks to her icy feet.

"We found her prone by the bedside in a tangle of bed-furniture," said the father sadly, "half-dead as you now see her. The crack of the breaking frame must have rouzed her, and she rolled aside an instant too late to be safe."

The purple-veined lids pulsed, and the mother renewed her endeavours. She was rewarded a moment later; the lids slowly lifted, and closed again.

But though a languid consciousness returned, it brought only the scantiest of memories.

"I heard a crack," whispered the white lips at Dr. Johnson's ear, "and felt a blow, and I knew no more."

I thought Dr. Johnson looked mighty grim. He sent me, with strictest orders to be on my guard, to the ordinary for broth, and he fed it to the child with his own hand. When she fell into a fitful sleep, he spoke sternly to Brewer Hosyer.

"The tontine must end."

"It shall end, sir. But I own I'm loath to give up the money; I'm pinched, and that's cold truth. My wife shall carry the wench into the country out of reach; and I'll do what I can to get the tontine parted orderly."

Johnson shook his head.

"'Tis your child's life. Pray be on your guard. If there's a human agent behind these accidents, be sure I'll be a mill-stone round his neck!"

The tontine was long a-breaking. I at last perswaded Sedge that the tontine might be broken by consent; though he could never be brought to think that the mortality among its members was other than a strange series of strokes of fate. Of Hiram Hosyer's importunities, and his brother's procrastinations, I only heard by indirection. Meanwhile, Sally Hosyer was gone out of London; Clem Sedge was at school and Bob Hosyer at the University. To all my enquiries after Breed Hosyer's affairs, I could have only one answer: that his credit stood high, his affairs were sound; men praised his prudence, that preserved his fortune in these adverse times, and the liberality of his lady, who had the spending of it.

The matter of the tontine was still in abeyance when Dr. Johnson and I went down to take the waters at Bath.

The well-known watering-place was thronged for the holidays. On every hand the Mall was crowded with gay duchesses, pretty pump-room girls, grande dames painted to the nines, and many a mincing maccaroni with a nosegay as big as a broom.

"Is not this pure, sir?" I addressed Dr. Johnson, unwontedly gay in mulberry and a new large grizzle wig. "Does not your heart bound to see so many pretty faces? Pray observe the fair sisters who approach us, attended by their court of beaux, and their duenna behind."

"I observe them," returned Dr. Johnson in a very particular voice. "They are not sisters, neither is she behind their duenna."

I looked again as they came closer. What was my surprize to see, handed each by an ogling gallant, Miss Sally Hosyer and my Lady her Aunt Hosyer! Stout Mrs. Hosyer scowled in the background.

It was the first time I had seen Miss Sally Hosyer on her feet. The girl was a raving beauty. Her towering head, picked out with plumes, was a replica of her Aunt's; her ruffles, like the older woman's, were edged with silver lace. Her skin was milk-white and transparent, and the warm colour came and went at every whisper in her ear. She carried her slim form proudly.

We bent low before the ladies, and they curtsied in a froth of taffety under-coats.

"La, Dr. Johnson," drawled my Lady, bringing her lace fan into play, "welcome indeed to Bath. Pray, sir, lend me your influence to bend this stiff sister-in-law of mine. Never doubt me, sir, she keeps this radiant creature penned up in lodgings, though I have begged her upon my knees, I vow upon my very knees, to come to us at the Priory."

"Nay, sister—" began Mrs. Hosyer.

"Now pray, dear creature, let's hear no more of the mill-pond. Do but be perswaded, and bring my pretty niece to the Priory. Here's Bob down for the holidays, he affects her prodigiously, I vow; do pray have mercy upon his transports."

"I don't hold," said plain Mrs. Hosyer bluntly, "with making a match between cousins."

"Dear joy, a match, sister? A match with a dowerless wench? Zut, sister, who spoke of a match?"

Mrs. Hosyer turned a dusky pink, but Sally only tittered.

"Ah, well, let it pass, sister. You'll come before the holidays are out. Only think, Dr. Johnson, that stubborn husband of mine has been brought to heel at last, and the tontine will be broke as fast as Lawyer Sedge can bring Clem to set his fat fist to it. But I daresay you will be by for the signing."

"At your service, my Lady."

"Your most oblig'd, sir. Do now, perswade my sister to bring her charmer to the Priory without delay. I vow Bob languishes; and cousins, you know, should love one another."

I regarded the painted blush on this unblushing creature with aversion.

"What is this painted bawd about," I cried angrily as the trio sailed off, "if it be not procuring for her own son in her own house! I never heard so infamous a proposal more plainly put."

"Infamous indeed," said Johnson, "and I could almost find it in my heart to wish her no worse than a procuress. But in two respects you wrong her—the boy is *not* her own son, and save for the crimson spots she is *not* painted."

"That white skin, not painted?"

"No, sir; this sunlight makes it plain, 'tis not white lead, but a substance even more noxious, to which the lady owes the whiteness of her swan-like neck."

I stared after the three ill-assorted Hosyer ladies. A bejewelled young rake had his arm about Sally's waist, the while he pinched her aunt's hand under her fall; Mrs. Hosyer's very back breathed helpless anger.

Who so willing as Miss Sally to compassionate a swain's transports? Some nights later I was wandering in the Spring Gardens with—but with whom forms no part of this history—suffice it to say, I was wandering in the Gardens at moon-rise. We were in shadow—I was in shadow as I rounded the hedge, and saw in the bright moonlight Sally Hosyer clasped in a close embrace by a tall young man. Unwilling to put them out of countenance, I stood silent. The embrace ended, the figures parted a little; when I saw that Miss Sally's inamorato was not only well-formed, but handsome and sentimental of face, richly cloathed, and in his first youth. For a moon-struck moment he stared into her lovely lifted face, and suddenly his grasp tightened.

"Sally," he said thickly; caught his breath, and spoke clearly: "Sally, my charmer, come away with me and make me the happiest of men."

Sally spoke in a small voice; her aunt's barbs had gone home:

"Without a dowry?"

"Without a shift," cried the young man passionately. "No one need know; 'tis no one's affair."

As to that he was certainly right. I slipped back the way I had come.

Whatever favours Miss Sally bestowed upon her young Adonis, she forebore to flee with him. I saw her upon the Parade the next day, mantling in a storm of compliments, and the favoured swain was no more than one of many.

Mrs. Hosyer, Lady Rivers that was, proved to be right about the tontine. Lawyer Sedge at last came down. He carried us to the Priory in his coach, and I for the first time beheld young Master Sedge, whom in Mrs. Hosyer's opinion nothing could kill.

There was reason for her estimate. I assessed Master Sedge as he sat opposite me in the coach, eating a gilded tart from a hamper. He had a large red face, and arms and legs like blood-puddings. He was not improved by having jam on his chin. He was six years old; his mental powers seemed to be less than the age would warrant.

At the Priory we found Hosyer and his wife and Sally already established, and a high tea on the table. They were making marchpane below-stairs; you could smell the ground almonds all over the house. Sally was munching on a piece. Clem Sedge, with a look of dumb determination on his fat face, snatched the dainty from her very lips, and bolted it. Sally just shrugged.

As tea was pouring, I looked about the richly appointed chamber at the group who sat there. Present in the room, with one exception, were all the surviving members of the Hosyer tontine, backed by their parents. I looked at Breed Hosyer, tight-mouthed and suave, his poison-white wife, Lawyer Sedge, bland and smiling, Hiram Hosyer, wary and ill at ease, his wife tense, Sally like a child, flushed and laughing, sharing the marchpane in her pockets with Clem Sedge. I thought of the mill-pond and the flux and the fallen tester, and a ripple ran along my nerve-ends. Where was Bob Hosyer?

Before I could ask the question, the door opened, and a beautiful youth in faultless buckskins strolled into the room. I had seen him before. 'Twas the importunate suitor of the Spring Gardens. Gracefully he saluted the company. A look of his eye, a private smile, brought the blood mantling to Sally's cheek.

Our number was complete. Lawyer Sedge proceeded to open the scheam for the breaking of the tontine. In brief 'twas thus: the tontine to be broken, and each member and his heirs after him to take his fair third of the sum; but the capital still to be in the hands of Mr. Breed Hosyer, and to be withdrawn only upon long warning. How this was to advantage Mr. Hiram Hosyer in his present need I could not see; but of all then present, he was most eager that the thing be done. My Lady was languidly willing, Lawyer Sedge not contrary-minded, Mr. Breed Hosyer wishing to have done with the matter. Sally and Bob, whispering in the corner, smiled assent, while Clem Sedge, his mouth full of marchpane, nodded dumbly. Lawyer Sedge pocketed his notes, from which to draw up the agreement fair, and we parted, agreeing to sign on the morrow. The last I saw of Clem Sedge, he was still stuffing his mouth with marchpane. . . .

The marchpane was the death of Clem Sedge. This time the gripes and the flux did his business. Mrs. Hosyer did her utmost, but in a frighteningly short time the child was dead.

Dr. Johnson strode angrily into my Lady's chamber. He found her eating marchpane while her maid did her head.

"Ma'am," says he without preamble, "you've poison on your toilette-table, and I beg you'll destroy it instanter."

She put down the marchpane hastily.

"I don't refer to the marchpane, ma'am, though indeed it serves as a handy disguise for a deadly dose; I refer to your complection-water."

She did not pretend to misunderstand him, but handed him a little box of white powder.

"Let it be destroyed," she said, adding with a sigh, "though never had I had so many compliments on my white skin, till by the advice of my apothecary I began the use of arsenick—"

"Your apothecary!" cried Dr. Johnson. "Many a Borgia passes under this guise today, witting or unwitting!"

"I have had qualms," said my Lady calmly, "for sure I sometimes think it was at the bottom of the ill supper in the nursery;

and sure Sally got a dose of it when she was here in November. It goes down fast; I think Sally uses it on the sly, or Hepzibah here—don't yank so, Hepzibah, you clumsy thing!"

"Clem Sedge has got such a dose of it," said Dr. Johnson bluntly, "as killed him."

My Lady quietly fainted, and not a lady-like swoon neither, for she slumped in a heap with her mouth open.

We left Hepzibah applying restoratives.

Dr. Johnson applied himself to tracing the history of the marchpane, but little enough did he learn. Every woman in the house had had a finger in it, even Sally and her mother; Bob Hosyer had been about the kitchen, exchanging banter for almonds; even Breed Hosyer, passing through, had paused to sample the confection. Dishes of comfits had stood in every room. Sally and Bob had filled their pockets. Poor Clem Sedge had been the only one to fill his maw.

These researches were cut short in mid-kitchen by loud screams of despair. We hurried towards their origin, and found the morning-room a scene of frenzy. Bob and Sally were missing.

No one had seen them since Clem had perished. My Lady was in a hideous taking, swearing 'twas all the fault of the little vixen, the— Her language astounded me. Mr. Hosyer said nothing, but he looked volumes. Mr. Breed Hosyer was cool as he ordered the grounds searched. The young people were not to be found.

"Then," says he, tight-lipped, "drag the mill-pond."

The brewer's wife upon this went into fits.

My friend looked unutterably grave. He was not content to lament supinely, but himself instituted another kind of inquiry, which soon bore fruit. Master Bob, said the groom, was off in the light chariot; but whether alone or accompanied he could not say.

Upon this we left the servants to drag the mill-pond, and took horse, the two fathers with us.

At the cross-roads we had the luck to encounter a carter who had seen the chariot. He had been forced to take to the ditch as the vehicle passed him in a cloud of dust; it was pelting north as fast as the horses could gallop, and the driver had a companion. More the carter could not say.

Upon this intelligence we whipped up our horses and rode Hell-for-leather out the highroad, Hiram Hosyer swearing he would horse-whip the whippersnapper to the parson, Breed Hosyer keeping his own counsel, Dr. Johnson gallopping ever recklessly in front. 'Twas by good luck that when we encountered a rough lad clattering along on an old plug of a horse, we drew rein to question him. He carried a scrap of a note in his hat-band. 'Twas addressed to Dr. Sam: Johnson:

"He has carried me off against my will. I am mortally terrified. We have turned in at the Swan. For God's sake come before it is too late.

S. Hosyer"

"The lady said," said the stolid boy as we set spur, "that you'd give me a guinea."

"Here's your guinea, boy," cried Breed Hosyer, tossing it to him, "the child's life is cheap at the price."

With no further word said we pelted on to the old Swan Inn.

The landlord of the Swan suppressed a grin as he pointed to an inner room. Thither we all stormed, and burst in in the nick.

I shall never forget that tableau—the table on the hearth spread with untouched viands and an emptied decanter—Bob Hosyer swaying beside it with the carving-knife in his hand—and on the floor at his feet, her garments disarrayed and her white throat bared, in a swoon like death lay Sally Hosyer.

It was Breed Hosyer who pinioned his son's arms; I had not suspected the strength in his wiry frame. It was I who took the knife from the boy's slackened hand.

No effort could restore Miss Sally; she lay like the dead. In the end we were fain to wrap her in blankets and carry her to the landlord's covered cart. We found, when we spared him a glance, that we had Master Bob on our hands too; he snorted stertorously with his head on the table, and no exertion could rouze him.

Murderer and victim we laid them side by side in the cart, and father and uncle rode beside. The look on Breed Hosyer's face terrified me.

There was little left of the night. Bob Hosyer was lifted like a log to his bed. I noted that Breed Hosyer settled himself by it, his grim visage never lightening; while a bewildered groom with a blunderbuss made his appearance beside the door.

Dr. Johnson never left Sally's side. Towards morning she came to herself and fell to screaming. Mrs. Hosyer fetched the sleeping-powders, but the box was empty; we were harrowed by the child's terror until she cried herself out and fell into a natural sleep.

By Dr. Johnson's desire we all met in the morning-room betimes. Tea and coffee was laid out, but truth to tell we had mighty little stomach to break our fast. My Lady looked haggard in the morning light; Mrs. Hosyer's eyes were red. Hiram Hosyer brought Sally in his arms; she lay on the sopha with her eyes closed. She wore a negligee garment of sky-blue silk richly laced. Clearly by giving her the garment my Lady had made her the best amends an empty head could conceive.

Last of all Bob Hosyer stumbled in, blood-shot of eye and heavy of head. His father stalked implacably behind him, and the groom and the blunderbuss made him look more than ever like a culprit approaching Tyburn.

Lawyer Sedge spoke. In twenty-four hours he had whitened and shrunk, and he spoke tonelessly.

"The document of the tontine can avail little now, but 'tis here, at your service."

Johnson shook his head.

"We must have signatures, and quickly. I have here a document that will serve till a better can be engrossed."

He read from a single sheet:

"I do hereby renounce my right in and expectation from the Hosyer tontine. It is right that I do this, as I now confess that it was I who killed—"

Bob Hosyer lifted his heavy head.

"—it was I who killed my late twelve fellows of the tontine—"

Bob Hosyer stood to his full height and folded his arms on his breast. The groom levelled the blunderbuss, and I tightened my muscles for trouble.

"—and I had in train to kill my cousin at the Swan, which was only prevented by the premature arrival of my father and my uncle."

Dr. Johnson dipped the pen.

"I am innocent!" cried Bob Hosyer desperately. "Father! Uncle!"

"Quiet, boy," said Dr. Johnson; and extended the pen to Miss Sally Hosyer.

The girl on the sopha lifted her lids and looked Dr. Johnson full in the face. Suddenly she snatched the pen and flung it to the floor, where it stuck and quivered like a thrown poignard. Then she fell back and went off in a swoon. It brought her thunderstruck parents to her side.

"Let her swoon," said Dr. Johnson indifferently. "She has a pretty talent of swooning. She swooned so soon as she had tipped the boat and drowned her cousins; you thought her in a swoon when she mixed arsenick with the nursery victuals; she swooned when the work of smothering her cousin and pulling down the tester was done; and she executed a very pretty swoon when we arrived at the Swan too soon for her plans, and her final victim, not yet completely subdued by the draught she had put in his wine, took the murderous knife from her hand."

"Will you believe this mad tale?" cried Mrs. Hosyer. "Who dosed the child with arsenick here at the Priory? Why should she first save Susan's life and then take it? How did she poison Clem, when they ate marchpane out of her pockets together? How could she hope to bring safely off the murder of a great strapping chap twice her size?"

"The child dosed herself with arsenick, in imitation of my Lady, for the complection; but being green at it got a swallow too much. She was well enough for the Lord Mayor's Show next day. As to Susan, 'twas her first venture; perhaps when the child clung to her, she lost her nerve. But it had to be done finally, lest Susan tell how Sally herself launched that unlucky voyage. The apothecary's sleeping draught that she had by her made it the easier. 'Twas the sleeping draught that was to put Bob in her power, once she had lured him away from prying eyes. As to sharing the marchpane with Clem, Miss Sally has *two* pockets; I think she never made a mistake as to which pocket *she* ate out of."

"But why? Why? Why? Is the child mad?"

She lay rigid as a statue. Dr. Johnson looked on her with regret.

"You may put it that way. These long and deep swoons are akin to what the learned call the catalepsy, to which misses at the age of the greensickness are much subject. Sally was just of that age when her sister died, and dying impressed upon her the misery of being without dower in this heartless age. After that she heard from her mother naught but the tontine. To drown her cousins was a sudden quick impulse, a surge of the will so frightful that a catalepsy followed. When it succeeded, and its companion impulse to arsenick the nursery viands, her succeeding murders became easier and more calculating. That of Bob was the hardest, had he not made it easy by yielding to her new-found power of charming, and forming dishonourable designs upon her."

My Lady had the grace to look put about.

"You may convince yourselves," said Dr. Johnson with compassion to the distraught parents, "as I was convinced, by the missing apothecary's powders. You have but to search the girl's room, you will find her hidden stock of both the sleeping and the complection powders."

'Twas done. Hiram Hosyer looked pitifully on the packets in his hand, and then on the still rigid girl.

"What is to be done?"

"I know not," said my humane companion, distressed. "How can I bring so young a maid to the gallows? Yet if she lives, who is safe from her wrath?"

"Give me," said the brewer sadly, "twenty-four hours before you move."

I looked once more on the exquisite countenance as her father carried her away. In the afternoon she came out of her swound, for again I heard her screaming. Then the apothecary's powders were brought into play, and the screams were stilled.

They were stilled forever. Her father's unaccustomed hand had mixed the dose too strong, and Sally Hosyer woke no more. Dr. Johnson grasped the brewer's steady hand, and looked into his tearless eyes.

"Sir, you are a Roman parent."

Bob Hosyer, who needed it not, had the tontine.

"Let uncle have his own again," he said. "I had liefer have had Sally."

[Every eighteenth-century tontine was an invitation to multiple murder; the Hosyer Tontine is typical rather than historical. Boswell and Johnson did not in fact visit Bath together in 1779; but I have not hesitated to place them anywhere, at any time, as the convenience of a plot might dictate.]

THE STROKE OF THIRTEEN
(*London, 1780*)

"Captain Donellan," said the soldier at the bar, "and gentlemen all, I assure you I was not asleep at my post; and to proof, as I stood there, *I heard the great bell of St. Paul's strike* 13."

The officers of the court-martial took this with blank amazement, which was broken when their senior broke into a roar of laughter, and the entire assemblage felt free to follow suit. A bull-throated sergeant laughed the loudest.

"Struck 13, my–," he sneered coarsely. "It struck 12, and I caught you napping, my dainty gentleman."

"You lie!" cried the accused soldier angrily.

The sergeant up with his cane and struck the young red-coat a savage slash across the face. In a trice the culprit had caught him by his thick throat, and the al fresco court was in confusion.

Two soldiers pulled off the raging young fellow. The thick-necked sergeant stood his ground with a sneer.

"That will do, Sergeant Thacker," the icy voice of the officer presiding dominated the tumult. "You have been heard, and your evidence will be attended to."

The rebuked sergeant saluted. Out of the corner of his mouth he grinned wolfishly at his adversary, who now stood scowling between his guards.

"As to the stroke of 13, Macdonald," the captain said to the red-coat, "never a clock in this world struck 13 save in dream. Your own mouth has condemned you. How say you, gentlemen of the court?"

"Guilty. Death," breathed an exquisite young ensign, fingering his ruffles.

"Death," grunted a thick-set lieutenant with a blue jowl, and yawned prodigiously.

"Guilty, death. Death," mumbled the other two officers hastily.

"Guilty, and so say we all. Private Allan Macdonald!"

The unfortunate youth stiffened to attention. He was a fine figure of a soldier, in the first bloom of his manhood, his red coat with its buff facings setting off his graceful tall form to perfection. The torchlight flickered on his tawny hair and marble-white, marble-handsome face. The mark of the sergeant's cane burned on one cheek like a brand.

I regarded the scene with emotion. A drumhead court-martial! At such stirring scenes might my days have been passed, as *Captain* James Boswell, had my scheam of life prevailed. But alas, 'twas mine to propose, my father's to dispose; so now, as *Advocate* James Boswell, I was in attendance at this military drama by pure chance. I had risen before dawn to ride in Hyde Park and admire, as it first stirred awake, the encampment of the military that graced the greensward there in that war summer of 1780. The light of the torches had drawn me, with many another early wanderer, to the scene.

As I saw it from the vantage-point of my light chaise, the picture is engraved on my memory. Before the white tent with its red top the officers of the court were ranged upon a crude bench, brave in full uniform, sashed, cockaded, splendid. To one side, a lanky soldier sat upon a three-legged stool and wrote with scratching quill. His desk was a tall regimental drum, and as he attacked a more difficult passage, the drum murmured with the impact. The young soldier stood death-still. The burly sergeant crossed his arms and sneered.

The presiding officer spoke. I much admired him. His powdered wig set off his fresh-coloured, handsome face, with the high nose of a soldier, the curved lip of a lover, and the well-opened, clear grey eye of a scholar. I envied him his red coat with gold braid, his officer's sash, his white breeches without a wrinkle, his polished gorget and silver-hilted sword. Just such a military figure would I have desired to be.

"Private Allan Macdonald!" he pronounced. "Insomuch as it is provided by the sixth article of the fourteenth section of the Articles of War that 'whatever Centinel shall be found sleeping upon his Post, shall suffer Death'; insomuch as you have been found guilty of that offence; it is the sentence of this court-martial that you be summarily shot. And since you are so adept at counting the strokes of St. Paul's," added the officer with macabre humour, "let it be at the stroke of noon, this very day, before Cumberland Gate, where the offence was committed. Take him away."

As the officers rose, my attention was diverted from the doomed soldier by a disturbance among the riff-raff and hangers-on.

"He's in a fit!" screamed a brawny milk-woman, pointing to a figure at her feet.

"Give him air!" cried a bony scavenger besmirched from head to foot, naming the commodity most to be wished for in his vicinity.

"Stand back!" commanded a watchman, jerking his staff.

"Ye'll murther the lad," cried a brawny Irish porter with noseless face, "for 'tis kilt he is already!"

I looked down from my chaise and saw the lad in question, fallen among them like a bundle of slops. He was a pretty boy, shabbily cloathed in someone else's waistcoat and breeches, a world too wide for him. In lieu of wig he wore a clout tied tight about his head, and his hat was fallen to the sward.

"Hand him up here, good fellows," cried I, "and I'll carry him to a surgeon to be blooded."

Twenty willing hands heaved the light form into the chaise, and the milk-woman threw his hat in after.

"Loose his headkerchief before he choaks," cried she, so positively that I complied with her wrong-headed admonition instanter.

By this means I made a discovery of a most interesting nature. No sooner was the clout loosed than down tumbled a cloud of palest gold ringlets—'twas no boy, but a girl of the most fragile and feminine beauty!

This discovery put me into a quandary. I could not abandon this delicate creature to some coarse surgeon, still less turn her back to the mercies of the rough crowd. I resolved to carry the child to Bolt Court and put her under the care of Mr. Levett the surgeon —the more that thither I was already engaged to go betimes to break my fast with my learned friend Dr. Sam: Johnson.

As I pulled up my chaise at Bolt Court, the sun was risen. So was not Dr. Johnson, who held strongly to the opinion, as I have elsewhere set forth, that the happiest hours of a man's life are those he spends lying in bed in the morning.

But Levett was stirring, the kitchen surgeon whom Johnson maintained in his motley establishment. The trembling girl, conscious now and sobbing, became his charge. As he ministered to her, they seemed to me most like some old woodcut of Miranda and Caliban, she so fair and young, he like an old *Brownie*, with his seamy, dusty countenance, his matted old dark wig, his swarthy skin, his square-toed shoes, and his ancient, full-skirted coat. As he brandished the hartshorn bottle, he might have been taken for some old-time alchemist, tanned like a bull's-hide in the fumes of his own crucible.

Miranda was sitting up in the great winged chair, still white as porcelain, but composed and calm, and *Caliban* was regarding his handiwork with satisfaction, when the door opened, and there entered the bulky form of the *Prospero* of Bolt Court—Dr. Sam: Johnson, philosopher, lexicographer, and detector of crime and chicane.

Dr. Johnson was now in his seventy-first year. That year was a rosy sunset for him, what the Colonists would call his Indian Summer. Never have I seen him so gay and good-humoured, so sociable and comfortable. Benevolence played on his craggy features and beamed from his piercing light-grey eyes. He shewed in his attire the unwonted haste of his rising, for his brown waistcoat was skip-buttoned, and his bushy grey wig, that knew the comb no more than a quickset hedge, rode precariously over one ear. But grandly unmindful of wig and waistcoat, the great Cham entered the room like a King to his courtiers, and he handed in his companion as if she had been a Queen.

His companion was a pale shrunken little old lady, ceremonially decked in scarlet of a by-gone fashion. Her face was meagre and her china-pale eyes were sightless. This was Miss Anna Williams, the blind poetess, who had long presided over Dr. Johnson's tea-tray. The tea-tray itself followed hard on her heels in the black hands of the servant Francis Barber.

Greetings were soon exchanged; but Dr. Johnson absolutely declined to tackle any problem fasting:

"Not a word, my dear," said he to the girl, "till you have taken your tea."

We were a strange consult, I reflected as we fell to, to take under our protection this fragile bisque statuette in the rumpled male attire. She sat rigid in her chair, and though she touched the tea to her lip, no morsel passed her throat. Taciturn Levett gulped bits of crust; Miss Willaims delicately groped up a bird-bite or two; Dr. Sam: Johnson drank tea in Olympian draughts, while I addressed myself to (O felicity!) the marmalade, and drank in, no less delicious, the girl's beauty. 'Twas a catalogue of perfection—arched brows over eyes of melting violet, straight nose gently retroussée at the tip, short upper lip, bee-stung mouth, chin a perfect oval, curls in a tangle like finest yellow silk a kitten stirs. No blood rose under the transparent skin; the girl sat like a marble statue on a tomb.

At last Dr. Johnson, replete with his seventh cup of tea, pushed back from the old-fashioned mahogany table.

"Pray, my dear, give us your story."

"You must wonder," began she, in a voice like a small silver bell, "what brought me to the soldiers' camp at such an hour, in such attire. I beg you will not think ill of me. I have done no wrong; and for my folly I am paid and overpaid."

Her voice faltered, and I thought she would weep, but she mastered herself and went on.

"My name is Lucinda Locke. My father is a rich merchant of Bristol. My mother died when my brother was born. That was fourteen years ago. Last year, in an evil hour, my father looked up from his ledgers and perceived that my brother was running wild about the wharves while I turned frump at home. He looked attentively at me, and concluded, how wisely I know not, that if Elizabeth Gunning the Irish beauty could have her choice of Dukes, so could I too.

"So to London we came, where Dukes abound. Soon I was surrounded by suitors; but none would do. The Alderman's son was a lout; the Duke's son was a rake; and Captain Donellan though handsome and accomplished, was twice my age, and had naught at all but his pay. Yet so runs the world, of all of them he has been the kindest friend to me.

"Meanwhile for my brother there must be a tutor to make a gentleman of him. A little Latin, and the genteel accomplishments, as dancing and sword-play, of which my father accounts sword-play first. My father is a direct man. He sets out to find my brother a tutor—where do you think?—at the *salle d'armes* of the great Angelo. He asks for a master of fence with a smattering of Latin; and he gets Allan Macdonald."

On the name her voice broke at last.

"Allan Macdonald is a gentleman," she went on, commanding herself. "His father was a cadet of Macdonald of Keppoch, who was ruined in the '45. Allan was bred a scholar and a swordsman, and maintains himself by his skill, and where is the harm in that?"

"Sure if I take you aright," remarked I, "he maintains himself upon the King's fivepence a day, or did until—" I stopped short, suddenly realizing in what peril the young Scotchman stood.

"My fault, my fault," cried she. "But for me he would still be a free man. I loved him from the moment I saw him, and he me. We were the two halves of one coin, the words of a song to its music . . ." The silver voice trailed off, and the violet eyes looked back into sunshine.

"I was sixteen," she remembered ruefully, "and I had never been crossed. I went to my father, and asked him to wed me to Allan Macdonald. I would know better now. He was turned off, and I was watched close; and Allan Macdonald took the King's shilling. But for Captain Donellan I should have despaired indeed. But he took Allan into his own company, and protected him from the brutality of the sergeant, and carried my letters to keep up his heart; and he was working for Allan's discharge. But the American war made a difficulty—and in short, gentlemen, I tired of waiting. So I sent a message by Captain Donellan, and bespoke the Captain's attendance for the sake of propriety, and dighted myself for safety in the weeds you see me in, and went to Hyde Park before dawn. But I came too late. The hateful sergeant had done his work too well; I came only in time to hear Allan Macdonald unjustly condemned to die—to die this very day at the stroke of noon. Dr. Johnson, you must make haste and save him."

"Why, my poor dear, what's to be done? Can I step between your lover and the muskets?"

"There must be a way—there *must* be a way!"

"There's the Leyden battery," pronounced Miss Williams in her old voice like the rustling of a leaf. "We may electrize the young man after he's—hem, when I assisted Dr. Gray, the noted Electrician, the Leyden battery worked wonders with deceased frogs."

"Tut, Miss Williams," said Dr. Johnson testily, "this is not a matter of frogs."

Miss Williams bridled, but said no more.

"I'll fix the captain a dose," volunteered Mr. Levett.

"You mean the sergeant?" I enquired.

"No, sir, the captain, him that hollos *Fire!*"

"Now, sir," said Johnson severely, "you've taken leave of your senses, to propose so coolly to give a soldier of the King a poison dose."

"No, sir, no poison dose, but say a great purge or a sleepy draught, shall occupy him otherwise till the stroke of noon be past."

"Foh," says Johnson, "there's officers enough in the regiment to hollo *Fire*, I warrant you. We must go another way to work."

"Allan protests his innocence," said Lucinda. "We must prove it."

"Prove it, my dear? In four hours? This is a labour of Hercules."

"And who so fit for the part of the Greek hero?" I enquired, viewing the great frame, the massive limbs, the large shapely hands of my friend.

"Well, well, as yet the cause of Allan Macdonald is Greek to me. But I will try to construe it. Pray, Mr. Boswell, you're a lawyer, detail me the case against him."

"Sir," said I, "the case against him is simple and damning. Allan goes on watch at Cumberland Gate. Midnight is scarce past when along comes Sergeant Thacker on his rounds. He finds Allan sleeping away at his post."

"He lies," cried Lucinda. "He hates Allan. He is wishful to lie his life away."

"What says Allan? Has he no counter-proof?"

"Only," said I, "the stroke of 13."

"Thirteen? How is this proof?"

"Sir," said I, "Allan Macdonald avers that, waking as he stood his watch, he heard the great bell of St. Paul's strike 13."

"And others heard it?"

"Nay, I know not."

"There's one, that's certain. Sergeant Thacker."

"Nay, sir, he denies it."

"So he would," cried Lucinda hotly. "Yet there must be a way to prove it. There *must* be a way!"

She started to her feet, all languor shed.

"Why do we sit here wasting time? Let us go at once!"

"Go? Whither?"

"To St. Paul's! To Hyde Park! To Allan! Anywhere, save sitting here while the sands run out!"

"Child, child," said Dr. Johnson mildly, "not in those garments."

"You are right, sir. I'll send for woman's gear. But there's no time to lose. Do you and Mr. Boswell go at once, and send me word where we may meet."

St. Paul's clock was striking 9 as we entered Hyde Park Corner. A small bandy-legged sentry admitted us to the park without parley.

'Twas a sight to warm the blood. The conical red-topped white tents, the showy uniforms, the stands of arms, the waving standards, the park of artillery, the rows of picketed horses, and all the other paraphernalia of military life sparkled in the sunshine on the greensward and shimmered under the broad shade of the trees.

"A camp," observed Johnson sententiously, "is one of the great scenes of human life."

'Twas so indeed. Here a gallant grenadier in sugar-loaf cap dallies with some trim milliner's apprentice. There a sutler's booth displays a board "Pool's intire Butt Beer. Fine Ale and Amber," and the soldiers gather round. Hard by, the beautiful Duchess of Devonshire, clad *en militaire*, epauletted and cockaded, stands siege of a dozen red coats.

Soon we drew rein before the tent of the court-martial. 'Twas a brave sight in full sun, with the company standard waving before it, and the red of its peak repeated in a bed of flowers sparkling beside it like a pool of blood, a wave of full-blooded ruffled blooms like scarlet silk, with blackness at the heart.

Before the tent sat Captain Donellan. His cockaded hat lay upon the bench beside him. His waistcoat was unbuttoned; he wore a red flower over his ear, and sat reading upon an octavo in red leather.

When we presented ourselves, the Captain was eager to welcome us. He had heard of *Dictionary* Johnson. He must needs display his domain, and Dr. Johnson willingly observed the little niceties of life in the field. He much admired the patent camp bed and the chair that folded so neatly, the ingenious writing-stand and the rack of books. As was his wont, he lingered to read the titles, holding one book after another close to his near-sighted eyes and muttering: a Shakespeare, a Pope, Wolfe's *Instructions*, Dodd's *Sermons*, Linnaeus' *Genera Plantarum*, the physical volumes of Mead.

As we withdrew, to take our ease upon the bench, Dr. Johnson leaned with a grunt and picked up from the ground, where Allan and the sergeant had locked in combat, a little instrument of unknown use. 'Twas four sharp-clawed prongs bound together with a handle of cord. He extended it to the captain. The soldier's brows drew down.

"What's this instrument of torture?" he muttered. "And whence came it? If Thacker—" He broke off. "Pray, gentlemen, be seated."

As Johnson seated himself, he indicated with a smile the rippling pool of crimson flowers.

"'Not poppy, nor mandragora,'" he quoted from *Othello*, "'Shall ever med'cine thee to that sweet sleep that thou owed'st yesterday' . . . or should I rather cite Linnaeus? For which, poet or philosopher, do you give camp-room to this red-coat regiment?"

"For Linnaeus," replied Donellan, giving smile for smile. "'Tis sheer necessity that has set me a-gardening and a-soldiering in one summer, for I brought these with me from the East Indies, and I was unwilling to let their propagation lapse, even in the field. But come, sirs, how can I serve you?"

"You can serve Lucinda Locke."

Captain Donellan started.

"What do you know of Lucinda Locke?"

When he heard, he was filled with compunction.

"'Pon honour, Dr. Johnson, I would give £1000 that matters had taken another turn. But how comes Lucinda to be running about thus in boy's attire? Upon young Macdonald's misfortune, I sent her a message, on no account to keep our rendezvous."

"Then your message miscarried."

"'Sdeath and blood (scowling darkly), if my messenger failed me I'll have the hide off his back!"

"Well, well, sir, but will you serve Miss Locke and save young Allan?"

Captain Donellan lifted shoulder and brow, and slowly and ruefully shook his head.

"I have done all I could. The lad's offence, being in time of war, is not to be extenuated; he must be shot as an example."

"But if he be innocent?"

"Who can say he is innocent? When he leaned incapable, snorting like a pig? When he reeked of rum? When he was scarce to be shook awake?"

"Yet he avers he was waking."

"Waking? And heard the great bell of St. Paul's—"

"This is not impossible," said Johnson quickly, "if the wind sets right."

As if to prove his contention, at this moment the great bell gave voice: 10 o'clock.

"But he avers it struck 13!"

"And did it?"

"How could it?"

"That's to be seen. I shall make it my first point of inquiry."

"Well said, Dr. Johnson!" exclaimed Donellan, fired with hope. "For if he's innocent, he may yet be saved."

"I'll set about it. Where's Thacker?"

"Thacker? Thacker is cock-sure. You'll get no help from Thacker."

"Yet I'll see him. Where is he?"

"He's on duty."

"Where?"

"At the Hercules' Pillars."

"Happy he, to be posted at a publick house!" cried Johnson, smiling. "And where's the prisoner?"

"I regret, Dr. Johnson; you cannot see the prisoner."

"Yet (sternly) you'd not hurl him out of this world unprepared? I'll send him a man of God. Where is he?"

"At the Hercules' Pillars."

"Surely this is irregular?"

"He is committed to the nearest place of safety. Stay, this writing—" Captain Donellan scrawled a line on his tablets—"this writing will admit your man of God."

Our man of God was the Rector of All Hallows Staining, for whom we had done some slight service in the matter of the manifestations in Mincing Lane. We sent a sedan chair for him, with command to turn in at Bolt Court and fetch Lucinda Locke on the way. Then we betook ourselves to the Hercules' Pillars.

'Twas a snug little tavern at the edge of Hyde Park. The first sight that met our eyes as we entered the tap-room was Sergeant Thacker. He was alternating a pull at his ale-pot and a pull at the bar-maid, whom he held clipped about her ample waist as she sat on his brawny knee. His broad phiz had a hard shine, and he breathed heavily through his nose. His armament was set by, his waistcoat gapped unbuttoned. Opposite him, grinning into a pot of ale, sat a skinny soldier as unbuttoned as he.

We made bold to stand them a fresh pot. The bar-maid flounced off to fetch it. At the prospect the grins broadened, but a scowl superseded when we named Allan Macdonald.

"Him? *Gentleman* Macdonald?" grunted the sergeant. "He'll come to no good in the ranks—so I said to Captain Donellan."

"And so it fell out," concurred his red-coated toady.

The sergeant glowered with a sense of grievance.

"Handle him easy, says the captain, he's a gentleman. Ho! A gentleman! I found means to harden him up, I'll lay my davy—there's no place for a gentleman in *my* squad, so there isn't."

"Aye, Ned, so there isn't," seconded his chorus.

"'Stow your jaw! But he'd a lily liver, did young Macdonald. Sleeping on sentry-go! Cry for your Nannie, do, says I. Well, I'm rid of him, or shall be within the day."

The callous brute took a long swig at his pot and exhaled with satisfaction.

"You're certain he slept?" Dr. Johnson put it to him.

Thacker looked my venerable companion flat in the eye.

"Aye, I'm certain, and I'll thank you to mind your business, old square-toes."

"Aye, mind your business, old put, for the sergeant is certain, and so am I."

Dr. Johnson ignored the double affront.

"You at least were waking, sergeant—did Paul's clock strike 13?"

"What a pox," cries the sergeant rudely, "has all the world gone mad? When did any man ever hear tell of a clock that could strike 13? No, sir. I counted the strokes, it being then time for my rounds; and the number of strokes was 12."

"It was so," chimed in the grinning soldier, "for so did I count 'em too, more by token I had just flung the captain's note over the young lady's gate, and as I came away Paul's clock struck 12 as I'm alive; 'twas 12, I'll stand to it, eh, Ned?"

"I misdoubt you can count to twelve," his companion crushed him, "so stubble your whids, do."

"As a man stands watch under the arch of Cumberland Gate," I struck in, "is there never an echo might gather in the concavity?"

"Echo, concavity, bah!" cried the sergeant. "Give over! The pot's dry, and so am I."

As the pot was replenishing, the door was pushed slowly open, and there entered, looking mighty out of place, a thin, apologetic clergyman, our friend the good rector. He handed Miss Locke, now doubly beautiful in a pale gown of India muslin with round sash, like a good child.

Sergeant Thacker scowled over the rector's paper of permission, but he honoured it.

"This way, sir," said the bar-maid.

The rector followed her, and we boldly followed him. Nose in pot, the sergeant made no move to stop us as we all four descended the rough stone stair together.

We found Allan Macdonald in the ale-cellar, still in his red coat, with three of his comrades to guard him. Having broached a butt of ale, they were warmed with its contents. They admitted us with a right good will. Lucinda Locke went straight into the prisoner's arms.

"O Allan, Allan," cried she, "why did you leave me? Why did you 'list?"

The young soldier held her off at arms' length.

"*I* leave *you?*" he cried. "When you turned me off without a word of farewell? When you sent me back my gifts and would see me no more? What should I do but 'list and die?"

"I never, I!" cried the girl. "They were taken from me. My father tricked you. But let be, you shan't die. Captain Donellan is our friend, he'll save you yet."

"He'd best be quick," said the young Scot drily.

"He had all in train to obtain your discharge, but for the difficulty of the war," lamented Lucinda. "We were consulting daily, and you were as good as free. Why did this happen?"

"Who knows?" asked Allan gently. "I know I have done no wrong. Keep up your heart, my sweeting."

Lucinda clung without speech to the scarlet bosom.

"Pray, sir," said Dr. Johnson, "answer me a question or two."

"Your servant, sir. Ask what you please."

"Are you certain you heard the clock strike 13?"

"As I stand here. I was watching a sinking star, and musing upon Lucinda, and upon the long ill luck of the house of Keppoch. I feared to hear a *taisk*, a voice of ill omen at the midnight, and when I heard the great bell tolling I counted each stroke—'twas the unlucky number, 'twas 13, clear upon the dark air, and as it were coloured crimson."

"Coloured crimson!" I ejaculated. "Were you drunk?"

"No, sir. I hope I am a better soldier than to go drunk to my duty."

"Did you reek of rum?"

"There was rum issued, it being the captain's birth-day; but the captain's my witness I took but the one tot, he desiring me to pledge his health in it, and all the guard did the same."

Lucinda stirred and stood off.

"I must go to Captain Donellan. But first we have some business."

"Business?"

"For what do you think I came to the camp before the dawn? 'Twas for this."

She drew from her bosom a paper and a pair of rings and extended them wordlessly. The paper was a special license for the marriage of Allan Macdonald, bachelor, with Lucinda Locke, spinster. The young soldier gave it one glance, fell to his knee, and kissed her hand. She touched his red head tenderly.

"I tired," she said softly, "of sending you messages and having no answer, and hearing that the sergeant detained you at your duties. I resolved to have you at once or let you go forever. I came too late. They had you at the drumhead, and instead of the words of marriage I heard you condemned to die."

"Though I die you shall have me," cried the boy passionately, "since now I learn that that is your will."

"We have missed the rendezvous with my clergyman, by some hours missed it," said Lucinda, "but here's a man of God may tie the knot, and I beseech you, sir," (turning to the dumb-founded rector) "to make us one this instant, for there's little time left to lose."

So saying, she sank to her knees beside her lover, and the rector plucked out his book and began:

"Dearly beloved, we are gathered here together in the sight of God and this company . . ."

I looked about at the company. Never was a stranger wedding scene. The fat soldier slid down from the butt where he sprawled and shouldered his piece in deference to the solemnity of the occasion. The two on the stone step set down their pots and stared. The greenish, damp walls glistened in the half dark. The young soldier knelt like marble, the blonde lass lifted her head proudly. Only as she uttered ". . . till death do us part" did her clear voice break into a sob. When rings had been exchanged they clung together as if they had been made one indeed.

"Sir and madam," said Dr. Johnson, signing the paper as witness, "I give you joy, and if God wills it and I may prevail, for many years. I must be off; but if you be gone from hence before my errand is done, then look for me before Cumberland Gate."

So saying, he departed, leaving Mistress Lucinda to my charge; and as he mounted the stair in the half dark, the great bell tolled the hour: 11 o'clock.

Captain Donellan was not to be found. Lucinda was nigh despair as at last we turned our way toward Cumberland Gate. The ill-omened "three-legged mare," the triangular gallows of Tyburn, was in our eye as we neared the place where, saving a miracle, Allan Macdonald must die. The girl's knees buckled, and but for my support she would have fallen, as we heard from the park the long drum roll of the Dead March.

We pushed our way through the starers clustered at Cumberland Gate. There was Captain Donellan's company drawn up in full regalia before the rifle butts. Many a recruit looked greenish and sick, many an old soldier was liquored; but they stood stiff and sombre to see their comrade die. Only on Sergeant Thacker's greasy face was the grin still fixed.

I supported Lucinda forward. Behind us other footsteps came on, and then Mr. Levett stood beside us. He wore an old broad-brimmed hat, and carried a large green baize bag, to which with many a jerk and beck he invited my attention. Lucinda spared him not a glance. Her widened eyes were fixed on the firing squad, standing waiting with muskets a-trail, while Captain Donellan, hand to sword, waited too.

Against the towering twenty-foot earth rampart of the rifle butts, Allan Macdonald looked small and alone, though he stood proudly tall. His hands were free; I could distinctly see the wedding ring on his finger. I looked at my watch; it wanted but one minute to midday. Captain Donellan drew his sword.

At that instant Dr. Sam: Johnson, dishevelled and dusty, ran swiftly, though with ungainly motion, through the brick arch of

Cumberland Gate. As he neared the rampart, the first stroke of the hour sounded.

One!

Captain Donellan lifted his sword.

"Make ready!" he cried.

Two!

I found I was counting aloud.

"Wait!" cries Sam: Johnson.

Three!

"Wait for what?" cries Donellan. "He's waited long enough."

Four!

"For the last stroke," says Johnson.

Five!

"Five!" counts Johnson. "Give him his chance."

Six!

"His chance is over," says Donellan.

Seven!

"Present!" The muskets went up to the shoulder.

Eight!

With deliberate calm Dr. Sam: Johnson stepped into the line of fire.

"You'll wait till the last stroke," said he.

Nine!

"No!" cries young Macdonald, shaken out of his iron calm.

Ten!

"Quiet, boy," says Johnson. "Don't think I plan to be shot in your stead. Be still and listen."

Eleven!

Lucinda put up her hands to her ears.

Twelve!

Donellan raised his sword again, but Johnson did not budge. "Hist!" said he.

Unmistakable in the death-like silence sounded the stroke of—

Thirteen!

The silence broke in a wild burst of huzzas. Allan's comrades threw up their hats, threw down their muskets, broke their ranks, and danced on the sward. Somehow Lucinda got from my side and into Allan's arms. I found myself pumping my companion's venerable hand. Little Levett jigged with his green baize bag. Only Captain Donellan, white with rage, shouted in vain to quell the tumult. We left him shouting, and rolled away, piled somehow hugger-mugger into the chaise, for the wedding breakfast Allan Macdonald had never hoped to eat. I little guessed that the full story was yet to be told.

The scene of our rejoicing was the Hercules' Pillars, where one short hour ago we had seen a wedding and an eternal leave-taking; but this time 'twas in the best room above stairs. There Lucinda took the liberty to laugh a little and cry a little, all at once; and Allan took the liberty to cherish her in his arms for a space; while Dr. Johnson, Mr. Levett, and I exchanged mutual congratulations on the happy outcome. With a gap-toothed grin Mr. Levett turned out his green baize bag; it contained a prodigious Leyden jar. At this Allan merely looked puzzled; but Lucinda began laughing in earnest; and the cloth being laid, we all fell to.

We discussed a joint and a mighty veal pye, washed down with a bowl of Dr. Johnson's "poonch" in which we repeatedly toasted the wedding pair, rejoicing over the wedding lines, and over a new writing which Dr. Johnson now produced from his capacious waistcoat pocket.

"'Twas the best I could obtain, argue as I might, but it served."

'Twas writ in Dr. Johnson's elegant small hand, and signed with a scrawl by the commander:

> *If the Clock strike Thirteen, Macdonald is pardoned, and let him be forthwith honourably discharged.*
>
> GLOUCESTER
> *General Commanding*

"Discharged!" cried Lucinda. "All's to a wish!"

Upon that refrain they departed; and indeed from that day all was to their wish, and now they have seven fine sons and a handsome competency.

"Yet, sir," said I as, left to our two selves, we prepared a fresh onslaught on the veal pye, "here's somewhat that is dark. There's a saying, 'regular as clock-work.' How comes a respectable clock-work to so far forget itself as to strike 13?"

"Sir," said Dr. Johnson, "it does not so. Rather it strikes *12*, and immediately thereafter without intermission it strikes the next hour, namely *one*; which being summed is *13*."

"Yet why should it strike two hours together without intermission?"

"The reason is found in the nature of the striking mechanism," replied my ingenious friend. "A clock must strike when the minute hand comes full circle to the number twelve. Accordingly, it is so arranged that when the minute hand comes to twelve, it raises a catch which sets the striking mechanism going, and so many strokes result as the space before the next notch allows. When the time for the right number of strokes is past, along comes the next notch, the catch drops, and the bell is silent until after 60 minutes the minute hand again reaches twelve. Then again the catch lifts, the bell sounds and the catch drops again into the next notch. But if the notch between, say, twelve and one be *worn smooth,* then the catch does not fall, and the clock strikes 13."

"Remarkable!" cried I. "If Paul's clock lacks a notch, then at midnight it struck both *12* and *1*. But—"

"But?"

"At 1 it must then strike 2," I puzzled; something seemed at the finger-tip of my wits, almost within reach.

"This follows."

"And so with every hour following, till at *10*, 'twill strike *11*."

"*Sequitur.*"

"And at *11*—" I rose to my feet—"'twill strike *12* and *1* together, which is to say that at *11* 'twill strike 13—" I levelled my finger at my majestick friend—"and at *12*—'twill strike *2!* In a word, sir, a clock that strikes 13 at noon can *not* have struck 13 at midnight!"

"O ho, you have hit it!" cried Dr. Sam: Johnson, and putting back his head he gave way to his rolling Homeric laughter.

"Trust me, sir," said I severely, "this is no laughing matter. Am I to think that at your age and weight you scrambled to the belfry and tampered with this ancient clock-work?"

"Aye, sir," replied Dr. Johnson, sobering, "that is what you may think, for that is what I did. 'Twas easy to chip away the notch; but the climb to the belfry, that was the labour of Hercules!"

"At midnight, 'tis certain, that clock had struck 12?"

"'Tis certain."

"Then why did Allan Macdonald aver so stoutly that it struck 13?"

"Because musing upon ill luck, he fell asleep and dreamed it."

"Then he was guilty."

"He was guilty; but so vivid was his dream or vision, that he did not know it."

"And to save a guilty man, you tampered with the great bell of St. Paul's and lied to his Grace the Duke of Gloucester!"

"I would gladly have proceeded in a manner less drastick, could argument have prevailed, for I take it for certain that Captain Donellan's drumhead court-martial was irregular from end to end. But the Duke, being stupid, was stubborn. Only the stroke of 13 was strong enough to catch his fancy; so I gave him the stroke of 13, and saved Allan Macdonald."

"'Tis not like you," said I, "to pervert the ends of justice."

"Nor did I so; but on the contrary, I thus baulked, at the last second, as covert and wicked a murderer as ever I beheld."

"A murderer?" said I stupidly.

"Captain Donellan," said my friend.

"Captain Donellan?"

"The penniless captain, who wanted the heiress for himself. When Allan impulsively enlisted, he fell into his enemy's hands. The captain recommends him to his rough sergeant's dislike by the surest means, as a dainty gentleman to be coddled. The captain carries messages, and conceals them, and lies to the lady, all the time making himself her greatest friend and confidant. Then the lady resolves to wed her lover out of hand, and the captain is notified. He sees that only death will remove his rival; and he goes about to contrive that death as speedily as may be; and he would have succeeded but for the stroke of 13."

"Yet," I argued, "if Allan Macdonald had been shot for a military crime, how is that murder? For we know he slept upon sentry-go; and how is that to be imputed to Captain Donellan?"

"If Captain Donellan did not plan that it should be so, how did he send word of it to Miss Locke before the event? The sergeant counted the stroke of 12 *before* he started his rounds; but the messenger counted it *after* he had delivered the captain's note."

"Yet how can one man cause another to neglect his watch?"

"The ingenious Captain Donellan," replied Dr. Johnson, "is a disciple of Linnaeus. He grows the oriental poppy. With that cord-handled claw by his tent he scarifies the capsule of the poppy, as I have been told they do it in the East Indies where he served. He collects the gum that forms. To put a name to it, it is opium. I smelled opium in the affair when I was informed that Allan Macdonald had been hearing 'sounds coloured crimson,' as drugged men may do."

"Drugged men?"

"Allan Macdonald slept because he had been drugged with opium. 'Tis plain, he had it of Captain Donellan in that tot of birth-day rum, a coarse liquor well adapted to dissolve the drug and mask its bitter taste. Nor was it the captain's birth-day, I'll lay you a trifle, but the excuse served, and Allan all unsuspecting drank the sleepy dose."

"A dastardly plot!"

"And so simple and safe. 'Tis sure he'll sleep, and as surely the malicious sergeant will catch him at it, snorting like a pig and scarce to be shook awake—an eye-witness description, you'll observe, for Captain Donellan will make it his business to be watching to see that his scheam goes aright.

"Well, I've baulked the scheam, but I can't reach the scheamer. I fear another life, ere all be told, will pay. For Captain Donellan's too clever by half. One day, with help of Dr. Mead's physical volumes, he'll distil a draught more lethal still; and they'll hang him for it, mark my words."

And so, in fact, it fell out; for in 1781 Captain Donellan went on from Mead *On Poisons*, pag. 167, of *opium*, to Mead *On Poisons*, pag. 168, of *laurel water*, a very lethal draught; and then they hanged him. But that is another story—which may be read at large in the *Newgate Calendar*.

[Neither Dr. Johnson nor the ingenious Captain (who in 1780 was already married to an heiress) was in fact involved in the affair of the stroke of thirteen, an early-century anecdote to be found in Chambers' *Book of Days*.]

THE VIOTTI STRADIVARIUS

(*London*, *1783*)

The Viotti Stradivarius was detected by ear, a feat Dr. Sam: Johnson with his thickened and unmusical hearing could never have attained to; but so much does mind govern and even supply the deficiency of organs, that by mere ratiocination and knowledge of the world he was able to detect and restore, what the sharpest eye passed unseeing, the great Orloff diamond. The only loser by that night's strange work at Dr. Burney's was his daughter, Miss Fanny, whose little waxen figurine had to be destroyed beyond recall.

Eagerly I had accepted of that invitation to make one in a musical party of pleasure in St. Martin's Street. Men and manners are my study, and sure nowhere in London might one meet with such men, or such manners, as displayed themselves at the musical conversazioni of London's first musician and our very good friend, Dr. Charles Burney.

Behold me, then, James Boswell of Auchinleck, advocate and philosopher (if I may so stile an observer upon mankind) in my sky-blue sattin, attending, like a pinnace upon a man-o'-war, my stately friend Dr. Sam: Johnson. How well I remember the rugged countenance, the little brown wig, the massive figure, aye, the full-skirted snuff-coloured coat and the waistcoat with the brass buttons. How comfortably we were at home with handsome Dr. Burney.

We sat in his fine withdrawing room, once the study of Sir Isaac Newton. Every candle was alight, every sconce blazed, every prism shook with light. Seated by the fire, moulding a little waxen figurine with nervous fingers, mousy Miss Fanny was attired in violet brocade under tissue. I wondered much at such gaudy attire in the house of plain Dr. Burney.

The company that began to assemble was no great matter. First came the Bettses, father and son, violinmakers of St. Martin's Lane, small men, neat and cheerful, with quick brown eyes and respectful bows all round. Each carried an instrument, the father a violoncello, the boy a violin. The boy bore the flat cases with loving care into the little inner room adjoining.

Now came in Dr. Burney's favourite pupil, Miss Polly Tresilian, a Venus in miniature, a little perfection, with pouting red lips and her own yellow hair drest in the new round stile, set off with a baby's gown of clustering gauze, the colour maiden's blush. She was attended on the one side by her father, the portly rich jeweller of Cheapside, and on the other by his journeyman, young Chinnery, sandy and thin, and with eyes only for Miss Polly. 'Twas a trio known in every drawing-room and pleasure-garden of Mayfair.

But the trio had become a quartet. If Chinnery had eyes only for Polly, Polly had eyes only for the dark graceful young man who entered behind her. He wore his own raven curls clustering about a well-shaped head. His figure, though small, was well-proportioned and graceful, and set off by a quiet suit of gold brocade. His olive features were expressive, amiable, and radiant, and he bent his melting black eyes upon Miss Polly. He carried a violin in its flat case. Tresilian presented him with pride:

"Giovanni Battista Viotti, the wonder of the age! The sweetest fiddler that ever touched string! The favourite pupil of Pugnani, that has transcended the master! Honoured by Queen Marie Antoinette and the Empress Catherine! Yet now he comes to England as a simple fiddler, without fanfare; and had not my brother the lapidary of Paris sent him to me for a banker, he had been lost to us in the crowd."

Upon this encomium, the famous Italian looked mighty abashed and put about; he bowed low, and looked for a corner to hide in. Dr. Burney made him most cordially welcome, and I would have escorted him to the seat of honour by the fire, had not Miss Fanny drawn him to her on the other side.

"Pray, pray," I cried, "Signor Viotti, let us not delay, but give us a touch of your string!"

Upon this an air of waiting settled upon Dr. Burney and Miss Fanny, and all was unaccountably delayed, so that I was constrained to whisper a question in Miss Fanny's ear.

"You think right," she whispered back, "there is indeed a guest to come, none other than the great Russian, Prince Orloff, lover to the Empress, whose terrible thumb strangled the Czar, as the whisper goes. He is music-mad, and resorts to us much. But perhaps this is he."

A mighty thundering upon the door promised no less. The door swung open, and an absolute giant of a man crowded through. He stood not an inch under seven feet high, a man handsome, well-fleshed, upright, and magnificent. He was superbly drest in the French stile, and adorned as for a court birthday. He had a star of diamonds of prodigious brilliancy, and a shoulder knot of the same lustre and value. A picture of the Empress hung round his neck by a riband, set with diamonds of such brightness and magnitude that when near the light they were too dazzling for the eye, and made the lustres dim.

He made his greetings with an air and address shewy, striking, and assiduously courteous, with now and then a quick darting look that seemed to say, "I hope you observe that I come from a polished court?—I hope you take note that I am no Cossack?" Little Miss Polly positively took her eyes off young Viotti, and gasped, as the newcomer made her his bow, and favoured her with an ogling, half cynical, half amorous, cast of the eye.

She gasped again as she caught a first glimpse of the Prince's entourage: two great Cossacks who made up in the height of their fur hats what they lacked of Prince Orloff's stature. They flanked the door with folded arms and looked at nobody. Clearly they were to be regarded as furniture, most like the horses which waited with the Prince's carriage in the alley below.

Prince Orloff was mighty affable and complaisant. He and Dr. Johnson exchanged most respectful greetings. There was a brief flurry of bows as each ceded the other the place of honour, and then all subsided into silence and stared at the romantick Russian, while he stared back. This impasse was broken when little Miss Polly whispered a wish into Miss Fanny's ear, and she as ambassadress carried it to His Highness.

The little lady wished to see the miniature of the Empress a little nearer, the monstrous height of the wearer putting it quite out of her view.

The Prince laughed, rather sardonically; yet with ready good humour complied; telling Miss Fanny, *sans ceremonie,* to untie the riband round his neck, and give the picture into the possession of the Fair.

He was very gallant and debonaire upon the occasion; yet through all the superb magnificence of his display of courtly manners, a little bit of the Cossack, methought, broke out, when he desired to know whether the Fair desired anything else? declaring, with a smiling bow, and rolling, languishing, yet half contemptuous eyes, that, if the Fair would issue her commands, he would be stript entirely! At this Miss Fanny flushed, and hastily passed the miniature into my hands.

There was hardly any looking at the picture of the Empress for the glare of the diamonds. They were crowded into a barbaric setting of pure gold, and pendant at the bottom from a loop of gold hung quite the largest diamond I have ever seen, cut *en pendeloque,* long and lustre-shaped, and something of the colour of a ripe pear. Dr. Sam: Johnson blinked nearsightedly at the thing over my shoulder.

"This is a prodigious gem," said I. "Pray, your highness, has it not a history?"

"A black one," said the Prince carelessly. "'Twas stole from the forehead of a Hindoo idol by a rascally French sailor, and so passed by theft and violence from one scoundrel to another."

"Good lack!" cried little Miss Tresilian, "how if you should meet the three visiting Hindoo nabobs face to face!"

"But naturally I have met them," replied the Russian, showing all his teeth in a grin. "Mrs. Montague had the three Hindoos; Mrs. Vesey had the Russian Prince; naturally to maintain her supremacy, Mrs. Thrale was forced to have the three Hindoos *and* the Russian Prince."

"Oh, good lack," cried Miss Tresilian, pleased, "and what said they to the idol's ornament?"

"Never a word said they, but eyed it without blinking. 'Twas at their eye-level," added the Russian giant.

"You must keep a good look-out," said I, "against Lascars and darkavised men."

"Nay," roared the Russian giant, "let *them* look out for *me*. 'Tis mine, and so I will maintain, for I paid 200,000 rubles for it."

"So much?" breathed old Betts, and had the gems from my hand. He carried the thing under the mantelpiece lustres, and examined it with his glass to his eye, murmuring the while: "Nay, Arthur, I must get this by heart, I must fail of no detail, an account of this will be meat and drink to your uncle the Dutch merchant!"

Over his shoulder young Arthur regarded the precious thing with lacklustre eye. "Of what use is it?" he scoffed. "Can a man eat it? Will it cure the evil or the pthisick? No, Father, the famed Stradivarius of Signor Viotti is the treasure for my money."

"You say true," replied old Betts instanter, "and if I thought otherwise I had myself turned Dutch merchant and no fiddle-maker. Away, gross pelf!"

He yielded the blazing circlet carefully into the hand of Miss Tresilian.

"Welcome, gross pelf," murmured she with a rueful smile, and looked into Viotti's eyes, "for the tenth, aye the twentieth part of this gem would buy a life-time of happiness for two hearts."

The Italian pressed her hand, and together they gazed upon the famous Empress.

Chinnery bit his lip.

"Nay, then, let others see," he cried bitterly. He took the miniature. With professional attention he must needs examine the great stone through his lapidary glass, holding it in the glow of the mantelpiece sconces and turning it this way and that. Prince Orloff seized the occasion to murmur a word in Miss Tresilian's ear; clearly a Cossack compliment, for she mantled and shrank, and Viotti straightened his shoulders to glare at his highborn vis-à-vis.

Then Miss Fanny took the ornament again carefully in hand, and passed the riband over the bent head of the Russian giant. He settled the miniature in its frame of diamonds complacently against his massive chest.

"But come," I cried, "let us delay no longer to look upon the Prince of fiddles, the famed Stradivari of Viotti."

Viotti bowed, and fetched it from the inner room where our effects lay.

"You must know," said he, opening the clasps and revealing in the silk-lined flat case a violin-shape swathed in silk, "that Antonio Stradivari lived and worked at Cremona more than fifty years, and made many superb violins; but mine is the greatest of them all." He loosed it from its silk, and gave it into the eager hands of young Betts. All clustered about to view this second wonder.

"'Tis a giant among fiddles!" cried young Betts—"even as [bowing] Viotti is a giant among fiddlers."

"What minuscule holes," said I, examining the graceful curved incisions, like an S, in the face of the instrument, "how does one get inside?"

"Minuscule!" cried young Betts, "they are quite the largest I have ever beheld."

"That is so," said Viotti, "it is to this grandeur of dimension that I attribute my instrument's grandeur of tone. Old Stradivari never quite repeated it; makers think that to make so large an incision, the grain must be right, or the face will break."

"I am of that mind," said old Betts; "and as to getting inside, one must take the instrument apart; failing which, he may use my new-invented instrument, which I use for adjusting the sound-post—" he displayed a specimen from his pocket—"you see it is curved *so,* and articulated *so,* and it goes inside with ease, *so.*" With his neat little left hand, he manipulated the ingenious implement like a conjurer.

"Remarkable," cried Viotti, "I must have one."

"Pray," said Betts, "accept of this one."

"Sir," said Viotti, pocketing it, "I am your debtor."

"Then you shall repay me," said old Betts, "with a tune."

"At your service, sir. But I see tea approaching—" the fiddler began to case his instrument with loving care—"I shall fiddle for the company after our regale."

He bore the precious thing to the inner room as one carries a child to the nursery; and we all addressed ourselves to the tea-table.

Viotti drank his tea sitting at Miss Tresilian's feet. I thought the lady's eyes roved a bit as long as they were tête-à-tête; but when

Mr. Chinnery came from the withdrawing closet and moved to her side, where he sat glowering and taking nothing, then who so gay, so mantling, so laughing and pert as pretty Miss Tresilian between her two swains? And who, when tea was over, pressed for a tune so irresistibly as she?

"I am all yours, ma'am," said the handsome fiddler, and fetched his violin.

Miss Tresilian settled her draperies at the harpsichord, Viotti brought down his bow, and I heard the storied Stradivari give forth a note as dismal and dull as ever blind crowder scraped out of his kit.

Viotti turned white, and set down the fiddle.

"This is not my violin," said he.

Dr. Johnson, to whom all musical notes, when not inaudible, are painful, picked up the instrument.

"'Tis no other," he said positively.

"I know the voice of my violin as a mother knows the cry of her child," cried Viotti passionately, "and this is not my violin. 'Tis a clever copy, by eye alone you shall not tell them apart—but be assured, 'tis only a copy."

He put it angrily from him. I took the rejected instrument into my hands, I weighed it, I shook it against my ear. All seemed in order. I brought it to the light and peered into the f-hole.

"See, see," I cried, "the label! The Cremona label!"

Antonius Stradiuarius Cremonensis
Faciebat Anno 1709

"I see it," said Viotti bitterly. "He who can forge a violin can forge a label."

The Russian Prince, condescending to interest himself in the fate of the Viotti Stradivarius, bent down to peer in his turn. His miniature, dangling, caught in Viotti's raven curls, and as he straightened again the pendant stone parted from the soft gold loop with a jerk. 'Twas Viotti who first felt what had happened; he brought the stone from his locks with an exploring hand, and extended it to its owner, with a bow.

His Highness's answering bow was all civilized—but as his eye lit upon the stone his roar of anger was all Cossack. What he held was a prism of white glass. Dr. Burney turned pale; Dr. Johnson murmured in my ear: "Here is an artist at substitution!" and His Highness began to hiss through his teeth in Russian. Consternation struck the company; and futile though the gesture was, by common consent we turned to and scoured the rooms, inner and outer. The Orloff diamond was not to be found.

"This is a matter for Bow Street!" cried Dr. Johnson.

"This is a matter for *me*," replied His Highness, shewing his teeth and speaking too softly. "I am my own justice. I shall expose this thief, and my Cossacks will kill him for me."

Miss Tresilian rose in horror.

"Let no one move," said Prince Orloff, still between his teeth. "We will sit here, till my diamond is restored, and—" he bowed to Viotti—"we make common cause, Signor—till the Stradivarius is restored as well."

Never shall I forget the next three hours. At first Mr. Tresilian tried to take the reasonable view, and was mighty prosy in respect to the hazard of jewel-thieves in his shop. But Prince Orloff grinned upon him without mirth until his voice dried to a trickle, and died away. Miss Fanny would have worked her beeswax figure, but 'twas not to be found, so she worked her fingers instead.

Upon this Dr. Johnson was seized with one of his strange rolling fits, and went about the room touching everything against the evil chance. Oscillating his head and ejaculating "Too, too, too," with tongue and teeth, he perambulated the rooms, both inner and outer. Often have I seen him thus in Fleet Street, touching the posts of the carriage-way in his absent fit. Tonight 'twas his humour to touch the under side of every thing, even the window-sills, in and out; and to tell the prisms of the lustres, every one. The self-imposed task was scrupulously performed before he returned to his seat by the fire, where he sat rolling and muttering in abstraction. Once Viotti opened the instrument-cases in the ante-room, but fruitlessly, for he returned to his place again in dejection. And again silence took us, and Prince Orloff's demoniack eye.

'Twas Miss Polly who finally broke the spell. She went off in hystericks.

"Pray, pray, your highness," said Miss Fanny in a small voice, "be pleased to take our parole, this is most unfitting for a young and tender female. Pray let the ladies depart."

"Why, ma'am," replied Prince Orloff courteously, "you may depart when you will—but"—the Cossack shewed his teeth—"you must leave your garments behind!"

Miss Tresilian wrung her hands, but Miss Fanny shewed better resolution.

"Be it so. My woman shall bring us others, and the ante-room shall serve for tiring-room."

So it was done. Though the discarded garments were stringently searched as to every seam, nothing of note was found except indeed that Miss Tresilian was revealed to be wearing the new female breeches richly laced, a practise which I shall recommend to my dear wife.

Miss Tresilian returned to us tripping in the hem of a gown of Miss Fanny's. Prince Orloff himself plunged his fingers into her soft hair, seemingly undecided whether as a caress or a punishment, and finding nothing there, not even a pad of wool, pronounced her ready to depart. Now a new question arose: how was an unprotected lady to make her way back to the City unattended?

"Let me be searched, and I will see her home," cried Chinnery.

"'Tis my daughter," put in Tresilian.

Orloff was sick of the sight of them. He spoke in Russian to his entourage, and while one stood on guard the other laid hands upon Chinnery and bore him off to be searched. The ante-room was the scene of the proceedings, and Prince Orloff stood by to see that no seam, no curl of the wig was missed. Chinnery returned to Miss Tresilian very white, and fat old Tresilian took his place.

"At this rate I will go too," cried Viotti, and passed into the anteroom.

"Come," cried Chinnery, and without waiting for his rival swept his master and Miss Polly down the stair and away.

Viotti was seething upon his return to the withdrawing room, and when he saw the girl was gone his temper went higher. He rushed to the door. The Cossack without so much as by your leave wrenched the violin-case from his hand, had it open in a trice, and with one hand ripped out the silken lining while with the other he roughly shook aloft the substituted violin.

"Nay, keep it," shouted Viotti in a passion, and rushed without it down the stair. Fussy little Betts retrieved the lining from the floor, and restored the whole neatly to the case, shaking his head over the violin the while. Orloff eyed him malevolently.

"Let you begone," he shouted suddenly. "Search him, and away with him!— You, too," he added, scowling wolfishly upon the trembling boy.

They were searched and gone, and all the instruments with them, and still we sat about the dying fire, Dr. Johnson swaying and muttering, Miss Fanny working her fingers for want of her beeswax, Dr. Burney in gloomy reverie, Prince Orloff pacing the room in agitation, the Cossacks immovable with folded arms.

Suddenly Prince Orloff came and touched Dr. Johnson confidentially on the knee.

"For what do we wait?" he asked softly. "For a piece of dead stone? 'Twas mine, 'tis gone. It is the will of God. Let us go home."

"Now I see, Prince," said Dr. Johnson, "that you are a philosopher."

"It is the will of God," said the philosopher. "Let us go home."

Next morning betimes I waited upon Dr. Johnson; but early though I was, one was before me. 'Twas Dr. Burney's footman, his eyes starting from his face. He stood in the front room twisting his hands before him. Dr. Johnson signed me to listen.

"Which when I heerd this housebreaker a-prying and a-scratching at the entry-way, sir," said the footman earnestly, "I ons with my night-gown, and ups with my blunderbuss, and lets fly, Sir."

"What like was the miscreant?" enquired Dr. Johnson.

"Nay, Sir, 'twas that dark, I never looked at 'un, but let off my piece without waiting."

"Was he not a black man?" I asked eagerly.

The man shrugged.

"All cats is black in the dark, as they say, Sir."

"What wore he? A banjan? A turban, belike?"

"Nay, Sir, I cannot say, he was muffled to the brow in something, and when the blunderbuss went off he legged it mighty spry."

"Did you not hit him, then?"

"Never a whit, for I fired in the air."

"'Tis a great pity," said Dr. Johnson thoughtfully, "for 'tis clear that the diamond is hid in that room, and the thief was forced to return for it in dead of night. Now had you scanned him, or marked him with a pellet, you might have known him again."

"Yes, Sir," said the man miserably, "I conceived it was my dooty, Sir."

"Very good, William," said Dr. Johnson kindly, "always do your duty, my man. Well, we must see what we can do. Pray, William, desire your master from me, to make the withdrawing room secure, and admit nobody, until I shall direct him further. Say to him, that as soon as Boswell and I have broken our fast, we shall be with him straight, and shall concert further measures."

Making a leg, the man withdrew, and soon the floating aroma of good India tea heralded Francis the manservant with our breakfast.

"Surely all is now clear," I cried in excitement, "I see it all. This olive-skinned, black-browed young man who calls himself Viotti has hypothecated Prince Orloff's diamond, and but for the vigilance of the good William he had already carried it in triumph to the hands of his masters the Hindoo princes."

Johnson swallowed a swig of tea.

"How do you make that good?" enquired he mildly.

"Why, thus, sir. Who is Viotti?"

"Why, Sir, Burney will tell you, Europe's rising young violinist, the favourite pupil of Pugnani, the fiddler who has played his way into every heart in Geneva, Dresden, Berlin, Warsaw, St. Petersburg, and Paris . . . and into one heart in London."

"Are you sure Viotti is in London?"

"My eyes tell me so."

"You judge over-hastily," I cried, triumphing to have so caught out my philosophical friend. "Who has seen Viotti? Have you? Has Burney? Who knows that this black-browed young man is in very truth Viotti, and not an imposter? Your eyes tell you, here is a young man. Mr. Tresilian tells you, this is the world's greatest violinist. Who tells ***him*** so? The man himself. But a man may lie. Letters from Paris. But letters may be forged."

"Yet what folly," suggested my learned friend mildly, mopping tea from the ridges of his waistcoat, "what folly to attempt the one personation a man cannot make good. 'Tis as if I were to strive to pass myself off as Johnson the equestrian. How long can I sustain the character? I must be detected the moment the company challenges me to mount and give an exhibition of my skill."

"Aye, sir," I exclaimed in excitement, "and so must he be the moment he puts bow to violin—unless he has the wit to extricate himself by pretending the sad lumpish wails he produces proceed from a violin bewitched, a changeling violin, a forgery. As indeed the instrument he carries must be a forgery, for how is a masquerader to come by a genuine Cremona? Nay, what need has he of a true Stradivari, who cannot play upon it like Viotti, be the instrument never so great? No, Sir, depend upon it, we have here to do with an impostor, come hither with no other object than to steal the great Orloff diamond from the Prince."

Johnson: "Surely 'tis a needless elaboration. A man may steal a diamond without giving himself out to be the world's greatest performer upon the violin, the haut-boy or the Jew's-harp."

Boswell: "How? How is one to take a diamond from a warrior seven feet high, unless by lulling him into security? For which, his easiness at the home of Dr. Burney is pitched upon. His partiality for music is known."

Johnson: "Well, Sir, say on. How did the pseudo-Viotti make off with the diamond after passing under the hands of the Cossacks?"

Boswell: "Nor did he so. He dared not attempt it. Hence his fit of passion in departing. He must depend upon his entrée at Burney's to carry it off subsequently from its hiding-place within the room."

"Why, Bozzy, you must consider," said my friend, peering into the empty tea-pot, "that our thief, whoever he be, was fain to gain entrée at dead of night, at risk of a blast from a blunderbuss. Is this your conception of the entrée at Dr. Burney's?"

"Perhaps passion warped his judgment. Or, it may be, the princely Hindoos his masters pressed him to the attempt."

"Pray, Bozzy," said my friend with asperity, setting down his cup with finality, "let us have no more of this romantick tale of the princely Hindoos, who in my belief know no more of the matter than the babe unborn. The diamond is to seek in Dr. Burney's withdrawing room, and the thief is to seek among those who were in it, so let's be up and doing, and leave the Hindoos to Mrs. Macaulay."

So saying, he clapped his old cocked hat on his little brown scratch-wig and set forth. I followed suit, and we set out for St. Martin's Street.

Passing, as so often before, with admiration under Temple Bar, whom should we meet but the very man, him who called himself Viotti.

"Well-met, Dr. Johnson!" cried the volatile foreigner, "well-met indeed, for I am come forth to seek you. They give you a name, sir, for a detector of villainies, and I who have suffered one indeed, beg that you will put forth your endeavour to restore my priceless Stradivari and detect him who has made away with it."

I looked with amaze upon this impudence, but Dr. Johnson received the young man with unruffled complaisance.

"Pray, Sir, walk along with us, and let us take counsel together."

I fell back a pace, the better to have the suspected young man under my eye, the while my ear was alert to every word my astute friend might let drop.

"Well, Sir," began Dr. Johnson, "where, then, do you lodge?"

"At Joseph Hill's, Sir, at the sign of the Harp and Flute, in the Haymarket."

"Oho, the violin maker! Here's a man who knows a good fiddle when he sees it! Pray, sir, how know you that 'twas your own fiddle you brought away from thence last night?"

"I played upon it, sir, and it was never sweeter. I played for a space of ten minutes together, and then I wrapped it in silk, and laid it in the case, and so brought it away to Dr. Burney's. No, Sir, the exchange was made under my nose as it lay in the inner room, and the priceless instrument somehow spirited away from thence."

"No such thing, Sir," replied Dr. Johnson. "Did one of those who were searched to the skin by the Prince's Cossacks succeed in smuggling thence so large a thing as your Stradivari? Disguised, perhaps, as a walking-stick?"

"I give you back your question," replied Viotti doggedly. "My Stradivari cannot still remain at Dr. Burney's. Those rooms were stringently searched for a stone no larger than a nutmeg. Did we pass unseeing so large a thing as a fiddle? Disguised, perhaps, as a hearth-brush?"

I jerked my head at this impudence, and muttered "Tschah" between my teeth. Dr. Johnson cast me a lowering look, and as we approached St. Martin's Lane he continued.

"Let us approach the matter by logic. Who will steal a violin? He who can play upon it. Who will substitute a forged fiddle? He who can make one. 'Tis plain: if the thief be not your landlord Hill—"

"Sir, sir," I ejaculated, "the most honoured violin-maker in London—"

"Then it can only be . . ."

"Hark!" cried Viotti, oblivious, and stood quite transfixed. "Hark!"

Dr. Johnson frowned, and seemed to strain his dull hearing. I heard it plainly—the tones of a violin, of particular sweetness, and played with a practised hand. Viotti's eyes seemed to start from his head.

"'Tis no other," he cried in a strangled voice, "I cannot be mistaken, 'tis my own Stradivari, and played by the hand of a master!"

I looked at the house whence the strains floated. The narrow door was ajar. Above it hung a gilded fiddle, and the brass plate bore the legend:

"JOHN BETTS, Violin-maker."

Viotti rushed through the door instanter, and we were constrained to follow. Like the lute of Orpheus, the mellifluous voice of the fiddle pulled us irresistibly into the violin-maker's workroom. 'Twas Arthur Betts who played. He held the shining fiddle like a lover, and the silver notes cascaded under his bow. Seated at his work-table in a litter of pegs and patterns, his father beamed upon him and kept time with his famous articulated instrument. Our tumultuous entry but redoubled his smile. He met the rush of the choleric violinist with a rush as swift, and enveloped him in an embrace.

"Signor Viotti," exclaimed he, "I give you joy! Your Stradivari is restored to you good as new. You have been made the victim of an infamous trick, Sir, but by my skill I have made all right."

Arthur Betts, his fiddling broken off, extended the violin.

"Do you set bow to it, Sir," he exclaimed, "and your heart will be at rest. Oh, Sir, 'tis the sweetest, the most responsive . . ."

Viotti, in an agony of impatience, yet forebore to snatch the precious instrument. Gently he accepted it from the boy's hand, gently he set bow to it and drew it across the strings, and it answered him like honey from the comb. He began to play. If Arthur Betts had drawn sweetness from the famous instrument, now it was brought alive. It wept, it danced, it laughed, it sang. Never have I heard such fiddling. Even Dr. Sam: Johnson uncreased his brow. He looked at my rapt countenance.

"Is this Viotti?" he murmured in my ear.

"None other," I replied; and even as the great violinist dropped his bow and caressed the violin in the cup of his hand, I realized that all my conjecture was vain, and the answer to both our riddles was still to seek.

"Pray, Sir," demanded Dr. Johnson of Betts, "how have you wrought this miracle?"

"You must know, Sir," replied the violin-maker, "that I was no more satisfied than yourself that a substitution had been effected. I desired to examine into the matter more closely, and to that end, as you know, Sir, I carried the instrument away with me. This morning I set it on my work-bench and opened it—and lo, the thing was made clear. Some enemy—jealous, as it might be, or desiring to damage the master's reputation, had with great subtlety introduced against the sound-post—a quantity of beeswax!"

He handed the substance in question to Dr. Johnson, a hardening wad of the stuff of about the bigness of a nut of Brazil. I peered over Dr. Johnson's shoulder as he turned it in his big shapely fingers. One side bore the grain mark of the sound-post; on the other, clearly impressed, was the mark of a finger.

"Beeswax!" cried Viotti. "Small wonder the sound was deadened!"

"How so?" enquired I. A new realm was opening to me.

"I will shew you, Sir," said Betts. From his work-bench he took the two halves of another instrument. "The sound, d'ye see, Sir, is made by drawing the bow over the string. But the sound is thin, and of no account, till it be resounded within the belly of the instrument. Now much depends on this strip of wood which lies in the belly, being made fast there—'tis by name the bass bar; and much depends on this peg which joins top and bottom. This peg we call the sound-post, and 'tis most particularly not to be meddled with. 'Twas just here, that our Vandal had loaded the Viotti Stradivarius with this pad of wax. How determined an enemy is he who takes such pains. Pray, Signor Viotti, have you ever an enemy in England?"

"None that I know. Yet stay, an enemy I have, so much is certain, for last night in my homeward way I was followed, and I feared a knife in the ribs."

"More like a horse-pistol, with a 'Stand and deliver.' Yet you came off unscathed after all."

"I shewed him a clean pair of heels; I can run with the best. Yet how have I earned such hatred? Who can hate me so?"

"Who," said Dr. Johnson with a laugh, "but another violinist?"

"Or," said Arthur Betts quickly, "a rival defeated in love?"

Johnson was staring at the lozenge of wax through the violin-maker's glass.

"I think," he said in an absent voice, "I think we may soon find out."

"How, Sir?" demanded Viotti eagerly. "I would give much to know the scoundrel."

"There is a way," said Johnson, "or my observation is much at fault. Let us gather tonight once more, in the withdrawing room of Dr. Burney. I'll engage him to receive us. 'Tis there I'll expose Signor Viotti's enemy; aye, and perhaps restore the diamond of Prince Orloff."

The musical trio strove to learn more, but not another word would Dr. Johnson say. They perforce consented to the rendezvous.

We left Viotti descanting upon the art of violin-playing, and Arthur Betts hanging entranced upon his every motion.

"Pray, Sir," I enquired as we made the best of our way to Dr. Burney's, "how do you propose to lay your hand upon him who tampered with yonder violin?"

Johnson: "Look upon this wax. See the print of a finger upon it. I will engage, with luck, to fit this print to the finger that made it."

Boswell: "Nay, how? Remember the thumb-print at Stratford, where you said that some other means than gross measurement must be found to fit a finger to its print."

Johnson: "I have found the means. I will put my finger—nay, his own finger—"

Boswell: "Or *her* finger."

Johnson: "Or *her* own finger—'tis indeed a slim one—on the miscreant."

Boswell: "I muse who it may be?"

"An avenging Hindoo," hazarded Dr. Johnson slily, "passing himself off as Viotti?"

"Why, no, sir, no avenging Hindoo could win such sweetness even from a Stradivarius," I owned. "Nor would any avenging Hindoo have an interest in harming even the first violinist of the age. Sure such an one had attacked Prince Orloff direct . . . Prince Orloff! Pray, Sir, how do we know that he *is* Prince Orloff? Or that yonder yellow sparkler is indeed a diamond, or ever saw the land of the Hindoos? Is not all perhaps a hoax?—the seven-foot hero and his blaze of brilliants, and Viotti's fiddle choaked with beeswax till it croaks again—"

"Nay, Bozzy, spare me this while!" cried Dr. Johnson. "Be not so finespun in conjecture. I cannot see that massive thumb that choaked the emperor brought to the finicking task of introducing a lozenge of wax through an f-hole with a hump-backed darning-needle, and there's an end on't."

"Yet Orloff works in my mind," continued I presently. "How if he has hypothecated his own diamond? Perhaps he has insured it at Lloyd's coffee-house, and will have its value again from the gentlemen there."

"Oh, the diamond," said Dr. Johnson. "Well, I have my eye on the diamond, never fear."

"Or perhaps," I went on, "Prince Orloff fancies his diamond, and would keep it. How long, think you, will it be his after the Empress's greedy eye has lighted upon it? How better keep it, than to noise after the story of its greatness the story of its loss?"

"At last!" Dr. Johnson breathed in relief. "St. Martin's Street!"

Dr. Burney readily assented to another gathering in his withdrawing room. A card was sent to Mr. Tresilian, and another to Prince Orloff. The Prince's reply was characteristick: "If it is the will of God His Highness will come." Mr. Tresilian, entertaining no doubts of the efficacy of his own will, as touching not only himself, but also Miss Polly and young Chinnery, sent a curt assent in the name of all three. All that remained was to make the withdrawing room fast and wait the event.

Once more the company was gathered in Dr. Burney's withdrawing room. Once more the candlelight sparkled on Sir Isaac Newton's prisms, and the firelight warmed Miss Fanny's slender hands, busy with fresh beeswax. Once more Viotti languished, and Miss Polly mantled, and young Chinnery glowered, and old Tresilian watched the three. Once more the Bettses, neat and respectful, wore smiles unchangingly cheerful. As to Prince Orloff, he was tranced in apathy, resigned in fatalistick Russian pessimism to the will of God.

"Pray, Boswell, be so good as to assist me."

I leaped to my feet with alacrity. Dr. Johnson handed me Miss Fanny's lump of softened beeswax, with the injunction still to keep it warm.

"Good friends," he addressed the quiet circle, "we are here for a double purpose, to detect the Vandal who tampered with Signor Viotti's Stradivarius, and to discover the whereabouts of His Highness's diamond."

"If it be the will of God," said His Highness.

"If it be the will of God," said Johnson solemnly. "The lesser puzzle first. Pray, Mr. Boswell, a lump of beeswax. Mr. Betts, oblige me by setting your fore-finger to the wax."

The violin-maker looked up at him with quick intelligence; he saw what we would be at. He pressed his right fore-finger to the wax. Arthur Betts followed, staring in wonder. Miss Fanny was next. Dr. Johnson scanned each imprint eagerly through a glass.

Now we approached the group about Miss Polly Tresilian. She graciously complied with my humble request.

"Signor Viotti?"

Quick colour rushed up his dusky cheeks.

"Have I tampered with my own most precious possession?" he began hotly.

Dr. Johnson shrugged.

"Mr. Chinnery?"

"I will not, unless Signor Viotti precedes me."

Angry glances crossed. Dr. Johnson turned suddenly upon old Betts.

"You, Sir, if memory serves you are left-handed?"

"Yes, Sir."

"Then touch your left fore-finger, and do not trifle with me."

The violin-maker shrugged, and touched. Johnson scanned the imprint, and shook his head. What did he seek? Or was this perhaps but a pretence, designed to force the guilty to betray himself?

"I am brought to a standstill, unless you, Sir—" to Viotti.

Viotti shrugged, and touched. Now Johnson turned to Chinnery.

The thin young man felt every eye, and rose slowly.

"Pray, Sir, touch."

"I will not."

Quick as a snake striking Johnson had the slim wrist in his grip of iron, and pressed against the fore-finger the softened wax.

Chinnery was white as his ruffles as he nursed his wrist. "What signifies this hocus-pocus?" he demanded angrily.

Johnson produced the lump of beeswax he had brought from Betts's shop. At sight of it Chinnery went whiter yet.

"This," said my friend deliberately, "that when you tampered with Viotti's violin"—he held the young man's eyes with his in a gaze deep and full of meaning—"when you tampered with Signor Viotti's violin out of mere *spite* and *jealousy*, you left your finger-print on the wax plain as a foot-print, and a finger-print so singular that none in this room but you could have made it."

Viotti rose from the girl's side, dints of rage whitening his nose, fists clenching and unclenching; but Tresilian stopped him with a heavy hand on his arm.

"I deny it," said Chinnery in a strangled voice, "make that good."

"'Tis easily made good," said Dr. Johnson, still engaging his eyes. "I have long observed the pad of the human fore-finger . . ."

"Holy Mother," remarked Orloff, his interest finally piqued, "what a man is this, that goes about peeping at fore-fingers! To what end, in God's name?"

"Why not?" said Johnson over his shoulder. "*Nihil humanum a me alienum*. Now the human fore-finger, in the inscrutable wisdom of God, bears a pattern, as it were an eddy or a spiral, that goes to one center where the pad is highest. Never have I seen a triple center, and only twice in my life a double one—once on the finger of the Rector of St. Olave's, and once on your fore-finger, Mr. Chinnery. Now the finger-print on the wax has a double center. Was it made, think you, by the Rector of St. Olave's?"

Chinnery stood irresolute.

"Come, Mr. Chinnery," said Johnson perswasively, "this is not a crime you stand charged with, unless loving a lady too well be a crime. I counsel you, give me best, and be off with you."

Chinnery seemed to make up his mind.

"You have the right of it," he confessed, "'twas I tampered with the Italian's Stradivarius."

"Then satisfy us," cried Betts eagerly, "how you contrived to introduce a lump of beeswax through the f-hole and that without the use of my ingenious instrument."

"'Twas done by depression," muttered Chinnery. Viotti ground his teeth. "I am indifferent deft, Sir, being a lapidary, and as to your instrument, I made shift to copy it, having in my pocket a sufficiency of silver wire which I designed braiding into a ring for Polly Tresilian." His voice broke. "'Twas all for love of Polly, I could not bear he should make music with her, 'twas his playing bewitched her."

"Good lack, Tom!" cried Polly, and ran to him.

Viotti uttered a round oath in Italian, but upon his threatening motion Tresilian pinioned him. Polly had her arms about Chinnery.

"Poor, poor Tom," she murmured, "I love you best, indeed I do."

"Then be satisfied, and be off with you," said Johnson sharply. Viotti muttered curses, and wrenched against the restraining arms of Tresilian. "Take my counsel, lad, with an Englishman 'tis a word and a blow, or he takes you to law, and so an end; but a foreigner will have it out of your hide. Be off, and look to your skin."

"I'll go with you, Tom!" cried Miss Tresilian.

"Not so, Miss, you'll bide. Now be off, young Sir, and repent in time."

Quickly young Chinnery touched his lips to Polly's hand, and was gone. Polly burst into tears.

"Unhand me, Sir," said Viotti quietly to Tresilian. "You have my parole."

"A pretty comedy, Dr. Johnson," said Prince Orloff languidly. "Now for the after-piece. Where is my diamond?"

"Sir," replied Dr. Johnson, "'tis in this room. Yet I do not choose to sniff about like a dog after truffles. I shall look in my head, and find your diamond. Pray, Dr. Burney, have you ever a bowl of *poonch?* Your downright English *poonch* is a great quickener of the intellects."

"Now, Sir," said I with resolution, "you shall not take me twice in the same springe. Trust me, gentlemen, in these exact words did my learned friend engage with Bonnie Prince Charlie that he would find his missing ruby in the bottom of Miss Flora MacDonald's punch bowl, and drown me therein if he did not know where the thing was all along!"

Dr. Johnson flashed me a look so imperious and full of meaning that my voice died in my throat.

"Nay, Dr. Burney, I do but jest," I added in a small voice, "pray let the punch-bowl be brought."

"With all my heart," cried Dr. Burney. As the punch was brewed I reflected anxiously what my venerable friend could mean with his carousing. Could he intend the thief of the diamond should become befuddled, and so betray himself? My eye lit upon Orloff, and I saw it all plainly. As the glass went round I set myself assiduously to drink with Orloff, designing he should become liquored as my friend desired. As to myself, I had no care if I could be of service to his scheams.

The chimes of St. Martin's told the hour round, an hour of toasts and pledges. I looked upon my princely charge. His countenance seemed to waver like a face under water. The moment is at hand! said I to myself.

I sought my learned friend where he stood by the punch-bowl with his back to the company, intending to impart this news to him. He held a fruit-knife in his hand, and seemed to be peeling a prune.

"The moment is unmanned," said I.

"How?" said he, dropping the prune-pit into his cup.

"Unmanned," said I.

"Alack, Bozzy, so are you," said he.

He approached Prince Orloff where he sat wabbling by the fire. The next to the last thing I remember is the triumph in his voice as he cried:

"My inebrious friend Boswell was a true prophet, your Highness. I have found your diamond—in the bottom of the punch-bowl!"

The last thing I remember is the rough feel of the carpet under my cheek.

I opened my eyes with difficulty in the morning light. Dr. Johnson seemed to be sitting at my bedside.

"How now, Bozzy," cried he with unwonted geniality, "still unmanned?"

"Yes, Sir," I replied sheepishly. "And how do all friends in St. Martin's Street—" memory began to return—"is Signor Viotti reconciled to lose his Miss and gain his Stradivarius? And has Prince Orloff indeed his Hindoo stone again?"

"He has, then," replied Dr. Johnson, "and the thief is much beholden to you for an hour's clear start."

I rose to an elbow in excitement.

"Pray tell me the story, Dr. Johnson, how came it out of the punch-bowl so pat?"

Johnson: "Because I put it there."
Boswell: "Where did you find it?"
Johnson: "Where the thief had hidden it to be carried away, in a lump of beeswax affixed to the sound-post of Viotti's violin. This is an old trick of the professional jewel-thief. He'll come into a shop, and snatch up a ring or a gem while the 'prentice's back is turned, and quickly with a lump of softened beeswax he has brought with him he'll affix it to the under side of the counter. The shopman may search him all day long, he'll never find the ring; and tomorrow comes in his doxy, she knows where the beeswax is, and will quietly pick it off and carry it away."
Boswell: "Yet which of Dr. Burney's guests was a professional jewel-thief?"
Johnson: "Not one of them; but two were professional jewellers, to whom the trick is known. Neither do I think it a plot, whether against the diamond or the Stradivarius. But put yourself in the place of the young lapidary. He desires the girl, yet cannot have her without money. He sees her turning from him to a dangerous and charming new rival. He is deft and bold, and seems to himself to have lost all that makes life dear. Into his hands is passed a diamond of 50-odd carats, slightly held to a frame by a loop of soft gold. He examines it under a sconce set with prisms much the same size and shape. Now the theft of such an object, to any other man foolhardy and without profit, is to him exactly a source of pelf. He is himself a lapidary. He can cut the stone himself, thus destroying its identity, and providing himself with valuable gems that can be gradually in the course of his master's business turned to profit. It is the work of a reckless moment to substitute a prism, and make the diamond his own. Fortune favoured him, in that Miss Burney and not Orloff restored it to its place about the neck of the Prince. Now the diamond is upon his person. He cannot keep it there; the risk is enormous. He must hide it. He remembers the jewel-thief's trick, abstracts Miss Burney's softened beeswax, and looks about for a place that cannot be searched, preferably one that he can later

come at with ease. The violins! Can he affix the diamond to the *inside* of one of them, where short of taking it apart it cannot be come at? He is deft and desperate; he will try. He chooses Viotti's. From this alone we might have concluded the Bettses were innocent; they would have pitched upon their own instrument. But Chinnery *would* choose Viotti's, not only to throw the risk upon his rival, but also because Viotti frequents his master's house; it will be easiest to come at. I do not think he would have blenched at shattering the precious thing to bits to come at the diamond again."

I shuddered.

Johnson: "Leaving first, he could not know how his plans had gone awry when Viotti angrily repudiated the changed violin, and left it for Betts to carry away and open. And when he lay in wait for Viotti and saw him sans violin, what could he conclude but that the instrument was to seek at Burney's?"

Boswell: "I made sure 'twas Betts who tampered with the violin that he might make it his own; and fobbed us off with a taradiddle when we found it in his possession."

Johnson: "I thought otherwise when I saw 'twas beeswax had done the damage. The jewel-thief's trick flashed into my mind, and I made sure that I had recovered the Orloff diamond."

Boswell: "Yet how were you sure that Betts was not the thief?"

Johnson: "Because he yielded me the beeswax cheerfully and without a struggle, which he had not done had he hid therein a diamond worth a Mogul's ransom. Yet I had not to guess, for the finger-mark with the double eddy promised to betray the thief with certainty."

Boswell: "Having discovered the thief, why did you let him go?"

Johnson: "Because I never doubted but that Prince Orloff spoke no more than the truth when he said the thief should die—and I could not turn the boy over to death, once I had discovered the diamond. He took the warning and fled for it; though 'twas most obliging in Viotti to be in such a mighty passion with him, and so cover my meaning."

Boswell: "You presumed on fortune, in letting him go before you had assured yourself that you had recovered the diamond indeed."

Johnson: "Am I so foolish? I stripped back from the under side only enough beeswax to assure myself that it contained the Orloff diamond indeed, before ever I left the sign of the Golden Violin." Boswell: "Pray, Sir, tell me one more thing: how did you account to Prince Orloff, for having found his diamond at the bottom of a bowl of punch?"

Johnson fairly laughed aloud.

"Easily. I told him 'twas the will of God."

[Everybody visited the Burneys—fiddlemakers and fiddlers, Viotti with his famous Strad, Orloff with his diamond—but not at the same time. Though the people are real, the events are fictitious.]

THE BLACK STONE OF DR. DEE

(*Strawberry Hill, 1771*)

"'Tis a strange kind of thief, my dear nephew," wrote Horace Walpole on a day in March, 1771, "that goes to the devil's own trouble to break and enter, and then goes away with nothing for his trouble, not even a golden guinea out of a drawer full of them. But stay, you shall have the tale from the beginning.

"'Twas Monday I had a courier from cousin Conway to tell me that my house in Arlington Street had been broken open in the night, and all my cabinets and trunks forced and plundered.

"I was a good quarter of an hour before I recollected that it was very becoming to have philosophy enough not to care about what one does care for, if you don't care there's no philosophy in bearing it. I despatched my upper servant, breakfasted, fed the bantams as usual, and made no more hurry to town than Cincinnatus would if he had lost a basket of turnips. I left in my drawers 270 £. of bank bills and three hundred guineas, not to mention all my gold and silver coins, some inestimable miniatures, a little plate, and a good deal of furniture, under no guard but that of two maidens.

"When I arrived, I found in three different chambers three cabinets, a large chest, and a glass case of china wide open, the locks not picked, but forced, and the doors of them broken to pieces. The miracle was, that I did not find the least thing missing!

"In the cabinet of modern medals, there were, and so there are still, a series of English coins, with downright John Trot guineas, half-guineas, shillings, six-pences, and every kind of current money. Not a single piece was removed. Just so in the Greek and Roman cabinet; though in the latter were some drawers of papers, which they had tumbled and scattered about the floor. A great exchequer chest, which belonged to my father, the Prime Minister, was in the same room. Not being able to force the lock, the philosophers (for thieves that steal nothing deserve the title much more than Cincinnatus or I) had wrenched a great flapper of brass with such violence as to break it into seven pieces. The trunk contained a new set of chairs of French tapestry, two screens, rolls of prints, and a suit of silver stuff that I had made for the King's wedding. All was turned topsy-turvy, and nothing stolen.

"In short, they had broken out a panel in the door of the area, and unbarred and unbolted it, and gone out at the street-door, which they left wide open at five o'clock in the morning. A passenger had found it so, and alarmed the maids, one of whom ran naked into the street, and by her cries waked my Lord Romney, who lives opposite.

"All London has fallen to reasoning on this marvellous adventure, and not an argument presents itself that some other does not contradict. I insist that I have a *talisman.*

"You must know that last winter, being asked by Lord Vere to assist in settling Lady Betty Germaine's auction, I found in an old catalogue of her collection this article, '*The Black Stone into which Dr. Dee used to call his spirits.*' Dr. Dee, you must know, was a great conjuror in the days of Queen Elizabeth, and has written a folio of the dialogues he held with his imps. I asked eagerly for the stone. Lord Vere said he knew of no such thing, but if found, it should certainly be at my service. Alas, the stone was gone!

"This winter I was again employed by Lord Frederick C—to do him the same service about his late father's (the Duke of A—'s) collection. Among other odd things he produced a round piece of shining black marble in a leathern case, as big as the crown of a hat, and asked me what that possibly could be?

"I screamed out, 'O Lord, I am the only man in England that can tell you! It is Dr. Dee's Black Stone!'

"It certainly is; Lady Betty had formerly given away or sold, time out of mind, for she was a thousand years old, that part of the collection which contained natural philosophy. So, or since, the Black Stone had wandered into an auction, for the lotted paper is still on it. The late Duke of A—, who bought everything, bought it. Lord Frederick gave it to me; and if it was not this magical stone, which is only of high-polished coal, that preserved my chattels, in truth I cannot guess what did."

Thus, in gay mood, wrote Horace Walpole to his nephew, Lord Orford; and 'twas Lord Orford who, taking a soberer view, brought the letter to Dr. Sam: Johnson. 'Twas his belief, that the thief who had missed his mark in Arlington Street, might try again, and succeed, at his uncle's Twickenham estate, the famous Gothick Castle of Strawberry Hill.

Dr. Johnson, concurring with this view, found himself forthwith whisked off to Strawberry Hill; and to my delight, for I had never seen the place, Lord Orford accommodated me also with a seat in his coach.

We found Strawberry Hill to be a little miniature imitation of the Gothick, with lath-and-plaster battlements and a smell of raw wood. Nevertheless, it had every Gothick appurtenance, a chapel a-building in the garden, a great garden-seat like a shell, an oratory with its niches, a hermitage under a bank. A little toy house across the mead housed Kitty Clive, late the darling of the stage.

The chatelain of Strawberry greeted us in the library, when I perceived to my disquiet not only that he had not desired our presence or our assistance, but also that it was far from welcome to him. Indeed he looked at me askance when Orford named me, and knapped his thin lips together with ostentatious and ludicrous determination, as who should say, "Not one word shall pass my lips until this man and his notebook are out of earshot."

"What the devil do you mean, George," he muttered aside to Lord Orford, "by bringing *ursa major*"—by this disrespectful designation he intended Dr. Johnson—"to Strawberry?"

Dr. Johnson, by good fortune, was engrossed at the book-cases, oblivious of all else, but I watched the little passage enthralled. Mankind is my study.

Mr. Walpole is a point-device creature with a faded kind of fineness to his countenance, and large eyes full of sensibility. He frowned pettishly upon his nephew. Lord Orford is higher than his uncle, and broader, and smells of Newmarket race meeting. His scalded red visage and his blank boiled eyes are susceptible of little change of expression, but a kind of grin broadened his loose mouth. He made no reply whatever, merely leered like a codfish, and after a moment our unwilling host shrugged, and dispatched a flunky to conduct us to our chambers.

"The Blue Bedchamber, George. The Red Bedchamber, Dr. Johnson. And for Mr. Boswell, as you affect the Gothick, you shall lie in the Round Tower."

I heard Orford laughing to himself as he retired to the Blue Bedchamber. He sounded rather as if he could not stop.

Leaving Dr. Johnson at the Red Bedchamber adjoining, I followed my guide the fifty-foot length of the Great Gallery. At the west end a noble Gothick doorway led by way of a passage into the newly completed Round Tower, which on this floor housed a handsome drawing-room. The flunky conducted me to the Round bedchamber above, on the two-pair-of-stairs floor.

I took a romantick satisfaction in lodging in the Tower. The windows were mere slits in deep embrasures. Opposite the bed hung a portrait of a gentleman in tilting-armour; he held his casque in his hand. Over the deep fireplace was Hogarth's portrait of Sarah Malcolm the Temple murderess, which he painted in Newgate the night before her execution. In her uneasy company I erased the stains of travel before descending.

I found a distinguished company gathering in the Round Tower drawing-room. Mr. Walpole named me to them rather as if I had been a slug upon his roses. To my intense satisfaction, I found myself greeting the noble company upon a footing of acquaintanceship and mutual respect. They were Mr. Walpole's neighbour, the handsome Duke of Argive, his equally handsome brother Lord Frederick Cammill, and Lord Frederick's wife, Lady Mary.

I stared covertly upon Lady Mary's sweet face. She was the relict of the notorious Lawrence, Earl Fetters, who for her sake murdered his steward, and was hanged for it. Suffering had stamped its mark upon her, but she held her head proudly.

To my mingled relief and chagrin, the Duchess of Argive was not one of us. She was the most famous beauty of the age. She had come to London a raw Irish girl, so beautiful she could not walk in St. James's Park without a mob attending her; she had married the Duke of Hasilton one midnight with a ring from the bed-curtains; and when she tried to obtain for their son the Douglas patrimony, among those who defeated her was your humble servant, James Boswell—but that is all another story. Now she was by a second marriage the Duchess of Argive—and what would she say to James Boswell?

"My wife will follow," the Duke told Mr. Walpole, "in the carriage. The boy is ailing, and engages her attention."

"I fear you will never raise him," said Lady Mary gently.

"Nay, ma'am, he blooms in Argive; 'tis but the air of London sends him into a decline."

"Pray, Mr. Walpole," Lord Frederick diverted the conversation, "has Dr. Johnson seen the treasures of Strawberry?"

"No, sir," replied our host, "he is newly arrived this past hour."

"May not he see them now," begged Lord Frederick, "and we will all assist in the perambulation, and thus expend our time until our table at cards is complete?"

I thought the Duke looked mighty *bored,* as the new saying is; but Dr. Johnson bowed polite acquiescence, and Mr. Walpole seized upon the proposal with *enthusiasm.*

A great fire burned in the gallery as we admired the paintings with which the walls were hung, and the antique marbles that lined the hall.

"Make way," cried a rich deep voice with a chuckle in it, "for still another of Horrie's antiquities!"

Into the gallery like a City Company's state barge surged Kitty Clive, the beloved actress, now a hearty ample woman of some sixty years.

Orford, up to this time sunk in the sullens, brightened at sight of her.

"Damme," he shouted, "filly or mare, 'tis all one to me! Have at thee, Kitty!"

He rumpled her, and had a box o' the ear for his pains.

"God bless you, Horrie," cried Clive, spying my philosophick friend, "God bless you for bringing us Dr. Johnson. Sure I love to sit next to Dr. Johnson; he always *entertains* me."

So saying, she greeted the philosopher with a hearty buss, which Dr. Johnson, who esteemed himself for his gallant attentions to the ladies, returned with interest.

I was assessing Mistress Clive's ample frame, her broad red nosing shining like the sun in her broad red face, her brocaded gown as red, when turning to me she greeted me with a great smacking kiss. She smelled of otto and sillabubs.

In the hubbub of greeting the Clive, who must perforce buss every man present, the Duchess of Argive slipped quietly into the gallery. She wore pale grey, her colour was high, she greeted no one.

"The boy?" asked the Duke quietly.

"He mends," she said, "he has purged, and he mends."

From the gallery we passed into the Tribune, which lay by the Round Tower. As the gentlemen stood back to bow the ladies through the door, Lady Mary, who stood nighest, made as if to enter. The Duchess touched her sleeve. Lady Mary stood still the length of a heart-beat. Then the colour stained her throat, and she drew back with downcast eyes to give her sister-in-law precedence. A little sigh escaped her lips. Behind the Duchess, Kitty Clive flounced through with her blunt nose at an even sharper angle than the beautiful Duchess's chiselled one, burlesque in every waggle of her draperies. Dr. Johnson permitted himself a faint smile, Walpole looked pinched, and Orford guffawed; but the Cammills ignored the little scene.

The Tribune was a curious barroco room, shaped like a square, with four bays. A star of yellow glass centered the ceiling. Here were housed many of our host's choicest objects of curiosity. We gazed upon the dagger of Henry VIII, the silver-studded comb of Mary Queen of Scots, and the red hat of Cardinal Wolsey. In a glazed china cabinet we came upon the Black Stone of Dr. Dee. Everyone, Cammills included, crowded about to stare at it. Mr. Walpole was exalted as a showman.

"'Tis my newest treasure," said he, "the generous gift of the Duke of Argive by his brother, Lord Frederick—"

The brothers acknowledged his bow, the Duke, I thought, a little grudgingly, Lord Frederick with that look of self-satisfaction which habitually adorned his handsome, rather vacant countenance.

"You must know, Dr. Johnson," continued Walpole blandly,

"that Dee was an alchemist, and made gold for the King of Bohemia; and into this gazing glass he was wont to call his spirits."

He took into his hand the tooled leather case, one face of which still bore, neatly affixed, a slip of paper with the auctioneer's lot number on it. Removing the cover, he displayed to our curious eyes a black object like a mirror, round and highly polished, provided with a pierced loop for a handle.

"Pray, Mr. Walpole," said Dr. Johnson, "will not you put this object in a place of safety?"

"Sir," said Walpole, "Strawberry Hill *is* a place of safety. We are not plagued, as Fleet Street, by light-fingered gentry."

"Or," said I, "Arlington Street."

I had for reply a freezing stare, as Walpole replaced the Stone and conducted the party to the library.

We were forced to admire this spacious chamber. A large window looked east, topped with stained glass, with a rose window on each side. The room was lined with books, arranged in Gothick arches of pierced wood. To them my learned friend devoted his attention, blinking at the titles in the candlelight.

I picked up from a bureau a book lying by itself, richly bound in morocco and stamped with the Walpole arms.

"Well, Mr. Boswell," came the thin voice of our host at my elbow, "what say you to my little Gothick romance?"

"Why, sir," I replied, "nothing, for I have never read it."

Walpole smiled sourly.

"This, Mr. Boswell, is an ignorance not invincible. You shall have the reading of this very copy."

"Do," says the Clive, "for you've never read its like. It consists of ghosts and enchantments; pictures walk out of their frames; armour is heard to clank, and helmets drop from the moon. Horrie says, it came to him in a dream, and sure I fancy 'twas a dream when he had some feverish disposition on him."

I accepted of the volume eagerly. With such a prospect in store, I regretted having pledged myself to take a hand at loo; I was in haste to be at it. Dr. Johnson excused himself. He never plays at cards, preferring to supply the vacuity of life with conversation; which failing, he betook himself to the book-cases.

We sat down, therefore, seven at the table, to our game. I was out more money than I like, and feeling as *bored* as the Duke by the curiosities, when our game was cut short by a distressing incident. Lord Orford was in ill luck. He sat mum-chance, losing steadily, taking his breath noisily between his teeth as he saw his guineas swept away. Luck was all with Lord Frederick.

"Pam be civil," said he, leading the ace of trumps.

Lord Orford held Pam, the all-conquering knave of clubs, and was thus debarred by the custom of the game from taking the trick with it. He scowled with senseless fury; a moment later he took a distressing revenge.

With a sudden roar he leaned forward and seemed to draw an ace from Lord Frederick's sleeve. Lord Frederick leaped to his feet, his blank countenance purple with fury.

"What kind of jugglery is this, my Lord?" he demanded angrily. "I should call you out for this."

"Pray, sir," said Walpole hastily, "be so candid as to overlook my nephew, you know his weakness."

Still roaring with laughter, Lord Orford was hustled away, and in perturbed silence the party broke up. The carriage rolled off with the ducal party, Lord Frederick 'squired the Clive in her homeward walk across the moonlit mead. Dr. Johnson was already retired to the Red Bedchamber with Barrow's quarto of Archimedes. Walpole mounted to his two-pair-of-stairs bedroom, and I was left alone by the fire in the great gallery to read *The Castle of Otranto*.

Having once opened it, I was powerless to lay it down. Long after all were wrapped in slumber, I sat in the shadowy gallery and read by the light of a single candle.

Through the stained-glass window arch the full moon spilled blood upon the floor, while a shaft of cold green assailed but could not conquer the shadows of the passage into the Round Tower. I liked the shadows little, and less as I read Mr. Walpole's tale. 'Tis of just such a castle, most dismally haunted, at once by the vices of the chatelain and the avenging spirits of his ancestors. From the wicked lust of Manfred the Lady Isabella fled. I read entranced:

"Where conceal herself? How avoid pursuit?

"As these thoughts passed rapidly through her mind, she recollected a subterraneous passage which led from the vaults of the castle to the church of St. Nicholas. Could she reach the altar before she was overtaken, she knew even Manfred's violence would not dare profane the sacredness of the place. She seized the lamp that burned at the foot of staircase, and hurried towards the secret passage."

Brave, intrepid soul! I read on:

"The lower part of the castle was hollowed into several intricate cloisters; and it was not easy for one under so much anxiety to find the door that opened into the cavern. An awful silence reigned throughout those subterraneous regions—"

A silence as thick reigned in the shadowy gallery. I permitted myself an uneasy glance about me, before I read further:

"—except now and then some blasts of wind that shook the doors she had passed—"

Was that the wind in the battlements of the Round Tower?

"—and which, grating on the rusty hinges, were re-echoed through that long labyrinth of darkness."

I could have sworn that somewhere a hinge creaked. I rebuked myself for phantasy, and continued to read:

"She trod as softly as impatience would give her leave, yet frequently stopped and listened to hear if she was followed. In one of those moments she thought she heard a step—"

Was it a step that I heard? I shook off the fancy, and took up the tale:

"Her blood curdled. She was on point of flight, when a door was opened gently—"

Was not that faint sound, the opening of the door to the Round Tower? I forced myself to read on:

"—but ere her lamp, which she held up, could discover who opened it, the person retired precipitately on seeing the light."

The impression was too strong for me. I rose and advanced my candle to the Round Tower passage. The weak yellow rays assailed the darkness and barely revealed—

A shadowy Presence. It stood motionless in the pale green moonlight and gazed towards me. It was clad from crown to heel in an antique gown, the cowl drawn forward and shadowing the face, from which sightless eyes seemed to burn.

For a moment I stood as if turned to stone. Then the Presence melted into the darkness of the Round Tower, and the heavy door swung shut. It wanted no more to impel me to activity. The great key was in the lock. I leaped forward and turned it. The midnight intruder was a prisoner.

I found my learned friend abed in his chamber, reading his tome of Archimedes by candle-light, poking his head so close to the candle as to scorch the front of his nocturnal headkerchief, with a smell like ironing-day.

"Well done, Bozzy," he cried approvingly when he had heard my tale. "Time was, when you would have conceived no other remedy, but to repair to the oratory and ejaculate Ave Marys against the powers of darkness. You progress, sir, you progress. Let us at once go look upon this apparition, and so prove it to be flesh and blood. 'Tis to be hoped," he added thoughtfully, thrusting his feet into his vast buckled shoes, "that your prisoner is not our host, night-rambling in one of his Gothick freaks."

Though forcibly struck by the possibility, I nevertheless gripped the poker as we passed along the gallery, and held it at the ready when Dr. Johnson swung back the massive door of the Round Tower drawing-room.

The chamber was empty.

Dr. Johnson tried the windows in the bay. They were all made fast.

The Presence had not been flesh and blood after all.

My hair stirred at the thought. For Dr. Johnson, 'twas his irascibility that stirred.

"Sir," said he scathingly, "I find you do *not* improve, but the contrary. 'Tis said, Mr. Walpole's book has set Misses in boarding schools to screaming in the night. Sure you lie under its spell. Did not armour clank, and chains rattle?"

"No, sir," I replied, "but I heard the wind in the battlements, and a step in the Round Tower, and the opening of the door."

"Why, then," continued my friend severely, "perhaps your apparition stepped from yonder portrait" (pointing) "and has gone again home into its frame."

I yielded to his mood.

"It may be so," I granted him, "for I own, that I have been kept from mounting to my chamber above, by the fancy that the portrait that hangs in it, he in black armour, might step from the frame to trouble my rest."

"Sir, clear your mind of phantasy!" roared my *commonsensical* friend. "My mind misgives me for Mr. Walpole's Black Stone. It lies exposed to every chance in yonder open cabinet."

"We must," said I, "remove it to a place of safety."

"My chamber is too easy of access. Pray, Mr. Boswell, keep it by you this night in your embattled Round Tower."

It seemed an idle precaution, against a visitant that could pass through walls, but I acquiesced. I fetched the stone in its case, and carried it with me up the narrow stair into my bedchamber high in the Round Tower.

The portrait in black armour viewed my proceedings. The eyes of the face, and the eye-holes of the casque, seemed to follow my movements as I laid the case on the antique chest opposite the bed. I turned the key in the door, divested myself hastily, and blew out the candle.

The full moon streamed through the narrow slitted casement, and fell upon the chest. I took a fancy to expose the magick stone itself to the moonlight. It shone with an awful dark steady gleam. Even after I had drawn the bed-curtains, through the slit I could still perceive the magick stone shining in the moonlight. It seemed to me that then, if ever, the spirits must enter into it. Mingled cloudily with these musings was the thought of the man in black armour descending from his frame to bend over me. 'Twas my last thought as I drifted into uneasy sleep.

The moon was still in the south window when I opened my eyes again. Motionless in its bright ray stood—*a figure in armour!* I strove to shake off the phantasy, and looked again.

'Twas no phantasy. The figure was solid. It stood in the bright moonbeam and cast a shadow across the chest. The casque was not in its hand, but on its head. The visor was closed, concealing who knows what? Between the palms of the gauntleted hands lay the Black Stone of Dr. Dee.

I swallowed, and spoke. My voice came out in a croak:

"In the name of GOD—" I uttered.

With a violent start, the apparition whirled. The speculum flew from its hands, and landed safely among the bed-curtains. With measured tread the armoured thing passed from the room. I heard the key turn in the lock, the door creak open, and a heavy step descending the stair.

With damp palms I huddled my night-gown about me, seized the Black Stone, and fairly fled to the Red Room.

"Pho, pho, Bozzy," said Johnson angrily. " You dreamt it. 'Tis the natural result of Mr. Walpole's Gothick castle, and his Gothick romance, and his magick stone. Let us hear no more on't."

Nevertheless, he afforded me the half of his bed, and there I passed the night, with the Black Stone thrust up into the tester.

When I awoke, the sun was high. I found the company dispersed. Horace Walpole was feeding his bantams. Lord Orford was not to be seen. Dr. Johnson was in the wash-house engaged in experiments in natural philosophy.

The object of his study was the Black Stone of Dr. Dee. When I came into the dark, damp-smelling wash-house from the spring sunshine, he was engaged in duplicating the magick stone from a piece of cannel coal, laboriously chipping and grinding away the surface, and every so often laving the rough object in a bucket full of water. I could not see why he persisted in saving the sooty water that overflowed, but save it he did, storing it up in a graduated phial, and only decanting it when a new lustration occasioned a fresh supply.

Ultimately his handiwork satisfied him, unsymmetrical and rugged as it was. His next care was to weigh the polished stone against the rough one. They balanced. He scowled, dissatisfied; but declaring his experimentation at an end, he restored the magick stone to its case and the case to its cabinet in the Tribune, discoursing the while of substances heavy and light.

Chymistry is not my study. I was full of determination to consult him upon the nature of the apparition which the full moon and the magick stone of Dr. Dee had conjured into the Round Tower bedchamber, but sought in vain to stem the eloquence of his learning.

Dinner was a sturdy buttock of beef, of which Dr. Johnson ate ravenously, declining to say a word. Walpole picked at a cold bird. Orford's boiled countenance grinned steadily as he depleted a loaded trencher.

After dinner we parted, our host to the offices, Orford upon some errand of his own, my friend and I to stroll the meads.

Our way led past the hermitage. This time we glimpsed another of the appointments of Strawberry—the hermit. He was a sturdy strong-built man, having a long white beard and a hardy blue eye. His dun-coloured gown was kilted up, revealing that he was clothed in skins; though he had so little sense of the part that he was hired to play, that he was wearing buckled shoes. He had come to the opening of the hermitage to gaze across the mead; when glimpsing us, he hastily slipped back into the obscurity of his den.

Upon this Dr. Johnson recited the following burlesque ballad of his own making:

> *"Hermit hoar, in solemn cell,*
> *Wearing out life's evening grey,*
> *Strike thy bosom, sage, and tell*
> *What is bliss, and which the way.*
>
> *Thus I spoke, and speaking sigh'd,*
> *Scarce repress'd the starting tear,*
> *When the hoary sage reply'd,*
> *Come, my lad, and drink some beer."*

These lines, he maintained, though written in mockery of Dr. Percy the ballad antiquarian, well suited the ridiculous Gothick fashion of the time, when every estate had its *grotto* and its *oratory*, its *hermitage*, and in it its *hermit*; being otherwise an honest rustick fee'd to sit within and clank his beads.

The sun was declining as we approached the Round Tower. The ruddy rays slanted across the mead and illuminated, a long way off, the sturdy figure of Mistress Kitty, issuing from her door, with her rustick petticoats girded about her, and in her hand a milking-pail. 'Twas a little landskip in enamel, and put my friend in high good humour.

Nevertheless, we had no sooner entered the door than he fell foul of our host about the hermit:

"Are not there in the world enough of the unfortunate, who want a dinner, and know not where they shall lay their heads at night, but Mr. Walpole must fee some idle lubber to sit about in his garden, because, forsooth, in times past the land teemed with idle lubbers?" he demanded hotly.

"What idle lubber?" asked Walpole blankly.

"The hermit," replied Dr. Johnson sternly, "he in skins, who decorates your hermitage yonder."

"Hagley has a hermit," I put in nervously. "A hermit is the refinement of the Gothick."

"A hermit is the refinement of flummery," said my friend angrily, turning on me.

"I am sorry that Strawberry does not please you," said Mr. Walpole coldly. "The chaise will be at your disposal in the morning."

I was aghast. We were dismissed, and we had failed of our errand. Dr. Johnson merely bowed.

"And," added Walpole, preparing to leave the apartment, "permit me to state, I do *not* employ a hermit."

"Not?" cried Johnson in excitement.

"No, sir. My hermitage is untenanted."

"My apologies, sir," cried Dr. Johnson, "and I shall be ready to ride in the morning."

Supper was a stiff and uncomfortable collation. Dr. Johnson cut his tea ration to a mere five cups, and withdrew early. Soon I was constrained to follow him.

He was not in the library nor the Round Tower, the wash-house nor the Red Bedchamber. At last I found him in the Tribune. The Black Stone lay before him. He stared upon it, and said nothing.

"Pray, Dr. Johnson, give over your care in this matter. We are dismissed, and must depart in the morning."

"Why, then we will depart in the morning. But tonight we shall resolve this puzzle."

"Pray, sir, how is this to be done?"

"I have put my endeavours, sir, upon the stone, which is the end and object of these manoeuvres. I can give but little better account of it—" (replacing it in the cabinet). "Tonight we shall approach the matter at its point of departure—the hermitage."

'Twas Dr. Johnson's plan, I soon learned, that we should give our attention to the proceedings of this hermit that was no hermit, by watching before his cell and following him whither he went.

"Thus, sir, we may see how he gains access to the house, how he goes on there, and what his object is."

Retiring early, accordingly, upon plea of our impending departure on the morrow, we left the house by a backward way, armed ourselves with rough staves from the wash-house, and took up our post concealed in the scallop-shell settle.

In the trees above our heads an owl mourned softly. On the two-pair-of-stairs floor Mr. Walpole's candle burned in his bed-chamber window. The air was soft and smelled of spring. We sat a long time in the balmy darkness.

Once the owl was startled into flight. 'Twas the hermit come out to gaze towards the house. He returned to his cell in a little space. Time passed with leaden foot.

The moon rose behind the house, and began to swing out and up in the southern sky. Mr. Walpole's light went out. Once more the hermit came to his door and gazed towards the now darkened castle. Once more he swept aside the doorway skins and re-entered his hermitage.

Still we sat in the shadow of the shell. Again time passed. Suddenly Dr. Johnson gripped my elbow. A light flickered in the windows of the Tribune.

"We have watched the wrong man," I whispered aghast. "The hermit sits harmless in his hermitage while another steals Mr. Walpole's Black Stone."

"Say rather, while we watched the front door, the false hermit has made off by the back."

"The hermitage has no back, save under the bank."

"Then he has made his way to the house, *under the bank,*" replied my friend. "Come, Bozzy, this is a thing susceptible of demonstration."

He rose, and boldly sweeping aside the skins, he entered the hermitage. The hermit was from home.

The hermitage, however, was not untenanted. Established on the pallet, as if she had been there a long time, sat Kitty Clive. At our entrance she surged to her feet.

"Back!" she cried. "Back, on your life! There is death in this place! Yonder poor man hath been carried to his village sick to death of the small pox. Pray, pray, shun the infection!"

I drew back in alarm, but Dr. Johnson entered unmoved.

"Prettily played, ma'am," says he. "Drury Lane never saw better. I beg, however, you'll hold your peace. I am resolved to have a word with this pox'd hermit."

"'Tis but a quiz," says the Clive, "there's no harm in it."

"Then, ma'am," says Dr. Johnson, "we'll quiz the quizzer; so pray, ma'am, hold your tongue."

Kitty was perforce silent, and again we took up a vigil. The moon silently shone in at the opening. By its light I studied the appointments of the hermitage, the one low door, the walls hung with skins, a carved wood Virgin in her niche. The Clive stared before her, and bit her finger ends. Dr. Johnson sat by her side in meditation.

Soon, however, a step was heard. In another moment, the skins on the backward wall parted, and the hermit stepped through the opening. In one hand he held a wax taper; in the other, the Black Stone in its case.

When he saw us, he took one backward step before Dr. Johnson seized his wrist in a grip of iron.

"I yield at discretion," said the hermit with a shrug, and set down his candle.

Surely I had heard that voice?

Dr. Johnson stopped not to parley. With a sudden mighty tug he tore away the long white beard and exposed the face beneath.

Lord Frederick Cammill!

Dr. Johnson took the case from his hand and extracted the polished black speculum.

"Pray, Lord Frederick," he enquired, "what is the secret of this stone, that you give it away without a thought, and within a season, like the base Indian, you must have it back?"

"Nay, Dr. Johnson," replied the hermit, "Kitty will bear me out, 'tis but a frolick."

Never have I seen a countenance so little frolicsome.

"Ay," put in the Clive, "a quiz upon Orford. He opened it to me last night in our homeward stroll."

"Ay, so?" replied my learned friend. "Nevertheless, Lord Frederick, there is more to this gazing-glass than meets the eye. Let us try to discover its secret."

My learned friend turned the gleaming thing in the moonlight.

"The secret lies not within," he mused, "for 'tis most certain, the thing is solid."

"How know you that?" I enquired.

"Nay, Bozzy," replied my learned friend, "to what end were my experimentations of the morning? Have you never heard the tale of Archimedes and Hiero, tyrant of Syracuse?"

"No, sir," replied I, ready to be enlightened.

"Sir, 'tis of a goldsmith, who had of the tyrant a certain weight of gold of which to fashion a crown. Now Hiero suspected the man for a cheat. Accordingly when the crown came home, he asked Archimedes, whether it were all gold, or dilute with base metal? Archimedes made shift to measure its gross content of metal, by immersing it in water and measuring the overflow. In the same manner he measured out an equal content of pure gold; which weighing against the crown, the crown was demonstrated to weigh less. Now as every substance has its weight, and gold the heaviest, the cheat was discovered. The Black Stone, on the contrary, balancing an equal volume of coal, was proved to be solid."

"Well, sir," said I, "perhaps you are to gaze upon it, as did Dr. Dee, and the spirits will come to it."

I scarce expected my learned friend would imitate the astrologer; but solemnly he gazed upon the stone, turning and tilting the shining surface in the eerie moonlight. Turn it as he would, the surface gleamed blank; no message appeared, no picture rose to view. The long silence grew oppressive.

"Well, sir," said the false hermit at last, "do the spirits speak to you?"

"Ay, sir."

"And what do they say?" enquired Lord Frederick with a well-bred sneer.

"They say, sir," replied my friend, "*None so blind as those that will not see*. Pray, Bozzy, hand me yonder leathern case." He took it in his long fingers, reversed it, and shook it. "There's nothing within it, that's plain to a demonstration. But there is something without."

"Ay, sir, this will be the auctioneer's lotted paper."

The slip of paper was as large as the leathern case, lightly but firmly affixed to it by glue along the edges. In the center was scrawled: "No. 8."

"Does not this seem a large expanse of paper," enquired my friend thoughtfully, "for so brief a message? But perhaps there is a longer message *on the other side*? Pray, Mistress Clive, lend me a pin."

Staring, the actress pulled a long pin from her bodice. Delicately Dr. Johnson detached the heavy paper by the edges, and reversed it. A breath came from Lord Frederick. I advanced the taper.

"Why, 'tis a letter!" I exclaimed. "Yet how comes it to shew no signs of transmission, as folding or superscription?"

"D'ye think it came by the post?" demanded Lord Frederick contemptuously. "'Twas fetched from over the water, most carefully concealed, by being sewed in the crown of a hat. Look at the signature."

I read it off: "*Charles Edward Stuart*—the Young Pretender! And writ to—the Duke of Argive!"

"So," said Dr. Johnson, "this is the secret of the speculum—treason in high places."

"I cannot deny it," said Lord Frederick with gloomy resignation.

I read off the fulsome phrases: ". . . your influence in our behalf . . . reward your friendship upon our accession to the throne . . ."

"Nay, Frederick," said Kitty Clive stoutly, "pluck up heart, man, this letter is nothing. The '45 is long gone."

"Alack, Kitty," said Lord Frederick, "'tis no matter of the '45. 'Tis all too new."

"Pho, a forgery," said Kitty scornfully.

"'Tis the Pretender's own hand."

"Then," said the Clive, "we must—"

She broke off with a scream. Never have I seen such a look of horror on a human countenance. Her eyes seemed to start from her head, her tongue clove to the roof of her mouth, as she pointed a trembling finger toward the opening of the secret passage, and strove to speak a warning. I turned my head with a thrill of awful foreboding.

"We must burn it," said the actress calmly; and as I perceived that the gloom was but empty, I felt her twitch the paper from my hand.

My chagrin at being thus tricked before my venerable friend was doubled as I heard him speak.

"Ay, let us burn it," said he calmly. "Pray, Bozzy, the candle."

Dubiously I yielded it. Dr. Johnson advanced it towards the letter; but before paper and flame met, Lord Frederick intervened a hasty hand.

"Nay, Kitty, bid me take it to my brother, for I have sworn to lay it in his hand; and the house of Argive will reward you well."

The Clive reached him the paper, but Dr. Johnson came between.

"Pray, Kitty," he cried sternly, "do you hold this letter safe for the nonce, while we scrutinize this fellow's proceedings. What do you say to a thief who parades about in masquerade, and leaves his booty behind instead of bearing it away to a place of safety? A thief who courts attention instead of shunning it? What do you say to the strange debility of the Duke's heir, which only assails him in London? What do you say to the proceedings of the next heir, the Duke's brother, who so far from making the letter secure in secret, and so protecting the Duke from attainder, plays the fool with it until it comes to light, and will not suffer us to burn it?"

During this recital, Lord Frederick's frame seemed to shrink.

Kitty Clive slowly rose and drew away from him. Without a word she yielded the letter up to Dr. Johnson.

"In Arlington Street," pursued Dr. Johnson, contempt in his eye, "the noble house-breaker lost his labour; save that by turning out the papers he made sure that the secret of the speculum remained undiscovered. In his own person he learned where it was deposited at Strawberry, and returned a-mumming by Mr. Walpole's new-built secret passage—"

"To think," cried the Clive, "that 'twas I that revealed it to him, and provided gear for his masquerade, and victualled him in the hermitage, in the belief that 'twas but a bit of play-acting with a laugh to follow. I should have been better advised; for Lord Orford is notoriously mad, and who puts a quiz upon a madman?"

"The secret passage was built with the Round Tower, and the hermitage at the same time, to mask its egress? The entrances lie behind the great portraits in the rooms of the Round Tower?"

"That is so, but pray, how did you know?"

"I said it in jest, the apparition was gone back into the portrait; and began to perceive how it might be true in earnest. From the portrait, then, Lord Frederick in his hermit's gear entered the Round Tower, meaning to fetch the Stone from the Tribune hard by. Listening from the secret stair, he heard that we proposed to sequester the speculum in Mr. Boswell's room, at the same time gaining from our talk a spectacular notion for his next appearance. From your theatre-chest you, ma'am, fitted him out to affright Mr. Boswell; on which occasion he took care, to awake Mr. Boswell, to leave his booty behind, and to depart by the door, lest he betray the secret of the passage. Pray, Lord Frederick, satisfy my curiosity: why did not you tear the paper loose then and there, and thus betray your brother at a stroke?"

"When my brother found I had given the thing away," muttered Lord Frederick, "*you fool*, cries he, *a paper was hid there, could be my ruin*. He told me without reserve, how he had thus saved up the paper against the Pretender's return; but he allowed me to think it was somehow concealed within the stone, and so I could never come at it."

"Ho ho," cried Dr. Johnson, "thy brother knows thee well, I perceive."

"I beg," said the false hermit sullenly, "that my brother may not hear of this. 'Tis ill enough between us already."

"Ay, sir," said Dr. Johnson thoughtfully, "I have seen how your lady suffers, to have another, not near so well-born, take precedence of her as Duchess of Argive. 'Tis a bird of ill omen, and so Lord Fetters found her."

"Pray, sir," I struck in, scanning the thing from a lawyer's view, "how could you hope that upon attainder of the traitor the estates could be yours, and not the King's?"

Lord Frederick grinned sourly.

"'Twas worth the risk. I have friends in the right places."

"Well, well," said Dr. Johnson, "a word to the wise, and I have done. These proceedings shall be our secret, as long as the Duke of Argive guards his new-found loyalty, and *as long as the Duke's son has his health in London as in Argive.*"

"Sir!" cried Lord Frederick, stung. "Do you say that Lady Mary—"

"I say nothing, sir. The boy's indisposition may have given hope for this contrivance; it may be part of it. I say only, if you tender your brother's friendship, tender also his son's life."

Lord Frederick's haughty stare was a failure; his eyes fell, and he bowed his head.

"I perceive," said Dr. Johnson, "that we understand one another."

[This "Gothick Tale" arose from the real letter with which it opens, and displays the real world of Strawberry Hill. Only the Ducal neighbors are fictionized. The Black Stone is still in England, but not (as some say) at the British Museum. For help in seeking it, I must thank Dr. Lasker, Dr. A. A. Moss, and Dr. Wilmarth Sheldon Lewis.]

THE FRANTICK REBEL

(*Chelsea*, *1777*)

"What! Boswell!" cried the strapping virago to whom I had just been presented—"the friend to Liberty! Come to my arms! I must infallibly kiss thee!"

Though I am not by custom averse from the kisses of the Fair, I own that the proffered caress daunted me. The nymph who had offered it was taller than myself, vast, and antient; she had the hawk's profile of a red Onondaga, and a piercing, maniacal dark eye. Before I could protest, I found myself engulphed in draperies and soundly bussed on both my cheeks.

"The friend of Liberty," she cried, "is the friend of America, and the friend of America is the friend of Patience Wright."

Her voice boomed like an orator's in the dusky halls of the Chelsea China Manufactory.

Dr. Sam: Johnson snorted.

"As for thee, Sam: Johnson," cried Mistress Wright, "surly monarchist that thee is, a kiss is far from thy deserts; but I will kiss thee in token of Christian forgiveness."

Dr. Johnson started back in horror. The potter's freckled boy snickered; the potter yielded to a fit of coughing. As the proffered kiss was bestowed upon the rigid philosopher, I could only stare at the extraordinary creature we had encountered. Friend to Liberty and friend to America I had always been; I glory in the appellation; but at that juncture I was not forward to publish my sentiments. 'Twas at the height of our unfortunate struggle with our fellow subjects 'tother side of the water, and I suppose in all London no other could have been found, besides this mad American, who would shout out rebellious sympathies in a voice that could be heard with ease clear to the other side of Thames.

Dr. Johnson had come down to Chelsea, not to bandy words with a rebel, but to try out his newest clay in the potter's kiln. Setting his little brown scratch-wig straight and working his lips in silent disapproval, he withdrew to his work-room with what dignity he could muster. Being for the nonce potter's devil, I followed, leaving Mistress Wright engaged in kissing the potter's boy, presumably for being in his humble way also a friend to America. I pondered much what such a flamboyant rebel might be up to in London.

I was soon to learn, and from none other than the head of the secret service. Mr. William Eden came himself to Johnson's Court, begging with agitation my learned friend's assistance.

"'Tis Patience Wright the waxworker," he groaned. "'Tis certain she's a spy, yet we can do nothing with her. Her wax-works are all the rage, and she is so great with her Royal Highness the Princess Amelia, and with even higher Personages, that we cannot lay a finger on her. At the Palace 'tis all 'Patience' and 'George' and 'Charlotte', she being a Quaker by religion and a Republican by sympathy; and I have it from the highest authority, the woman has had the impudence to rate his Sacred Majesty to his face about the American war. Upon this she was banished the Palace; but Queen Charlotte still inflexibly protects her, the while she communicates to Franklin in Paris."

"Foh," said Johnson, "what does a madwoman know that could advantage our enemies?"

"She is not so mad but there's method in it," said Eden, biting his lip, "and as to what she knows, she knows enough at this moment to foil all our scheams and lose us our colonies forever."

Johnson: "Then she must be prevented from communicating it."

Eden: "Yes, Sir, 'tis a matter the most serious. When you have heard all, I know you will lay aside your every occupation in order to serve your country."

Johnson: "Well, Sir, say on."

Eden: "Sir, the scheam was laid down by one whom I shall call General B——. 'Tis for a military campaign of the first importance, which shall divide the rebellious colonies so that we may reduce them at our leisure. Now General B——, though a brilliant soldier, is in hours of ease a rake and a man of pleasure. No sooner, therefore, has he come to town, but he takes into keeping one Miss Fleay, late of the stage, and sets her up in a house in Chelsea, hard by the pottery. Down goes Miss Fleay to Chelsea with her cook and her odd boy and her waiting-woman—and Mistress Wright, if you please, goes along to teach her modelling, at which the lady has a dainty hand. Miss Fleay thought the kilns of the pottery the attraction held out by Chelsea—but now it appears as if the presence of General B— was the true loadstone."

Johnson: "Well, and so Chelsea was all one idyll of true love and modelling in wax."

Eden: "Aye, and thence comes our danger. In an ill moment, General B—communicated his scheam to his companion, whose loyalty is above doubt; only to find too late that Mistress Wright, the frantick rebel, had over-heard all."

Johnson: "If the secret's out, how can I or any man mend the matter?"

Eden: "Miss Fleay took steps at once. She attached herself so closely to Mistress Wright, that the American was totally unable to communicate with anyone; having meantime sent an urgent message to me, revealing the situation. We immediately placed the spy under the closet surveillance, and I do assure you that she has as yet neither communicated nor attempted to communicate with anyone outside the household. But this cannot last; she must send a messenger to Franklin at Paris, or go herself, within this eight days, if this intelligence is to advantage the rebels."

Johnson: "Sir, I am no bailiff; I cannot undertake to watch this lady. I am deep in experimentation with clays; my friend Boswell is newly come to town for a frisk; you must seek elsewhere for a watch-dog."

Eden: "Nay, Dr. Johnson, the lady is encompassed by watch-dogs. Miss Fleay has augmented her domestick staff; Mrs. Wright's waiting-woman is one of my people, and the coachman, and the gardener's boy."

Johnson: "Then what do you ask of me?"

Eden: "Sir, in the words of the satirick Juvenal, *Quis custodiet ipsos custodes?* We must have someone on hand who cannot be bought. Furthermore, the lady has a wild and fertile invention, beyond the ken of any mere watch-dog. I would have you match wits with her, and intercept her communications no matter how slyly they are put forth."

I was eager to accept the commission: "Pray, Sir, let us do it. 'Twill be better than any frisk, and not so dull neither; and as to the clays, 'tis but a step to your kiln at the pottery."

Dr. Johnson scowled; the ranting republican of the pottery was clearly before his eye. But Mr. Eden added his perswasions to mine, and Dr. Johnson, appealed to in the sacred name of his King, consented to sojourn in Chelsea till the dangerous week was past. For better obfuscation, 'twas given out to the gazettes that Dr. Sam: Johnson and Mr. James Boswell were gone down to Oxford upon a literary errand.

Mr. Eden's coach set us down in Paradise Row, Chelsea, without more delay. We found the frantick American calmly modelling the head of a Cherokee Sachem, pulling and pinching the softened wax. Her companion in the gracious panelled room was a lady, to whose charms I incontinently yielded my heart—Miss Flora Fleay, late of Drury Lane, tall, agreeably formed, with a countenance in which strong sense and caressing manners mingled. She greeted us with a suspiration of relief, Mistress Wright with a calm inclination of the head.

Seated hand in hand by the fire, an antient pair in Quaker garb greeted us not at all.

"Your servant, ma'am," says nearsighted Sam: Johnson, bowing to the aged lady.

"My old father and mother," said Mistress Wright, pointing towards them with a hand from which trailed plain ruffles rather the worse for draggling in wax. "Don't be ashamed of them because they look so—" the pair in question heard this extraordinary remark without moving a muscle—"they were good folks, they turned Quaker—"

I looked at the subject of this discourse. They were wax figures.

"They turned Quaker," Mistress Wright was rattling on, "and imbued me with their most excellent principles. I shall call thee Samuel."

"As you will, Mistress Wright," said Dr. Sam: Johnson wryly.

"Pray call me Patience. And thee, friend Boswell, what is thy name?"

"James."

"James, I desire thy better acquaintance. Don't despise these good old folk, they did well by their children, they would never let us eat meat, and that is the reason why we were all so ingenious. Thee has heard of the ingenious Mrs. Wright from America, I suppose?"

Dr. Sam: Johnson scowled like a thunder-cloud, as he did at every affectation of singularity; but Mistress Wright continued her discourse unabashed:

"And as to strong spirits, I do contemn 'em, holding that nothing so operates to void phlegm and clarify the intellects as prime lemonade, in a glass of which I desire you'll join me."

I thought the lady's offer rhetorical; when to my surprise she absolutely extracted from her capacious pocket a pair of lemons, and loaf sugar in a twist, and then and there compounded for the gratified philosopher a glass of his favorite regale. Dr. Sam: Johnson assisted at the mysteries with complaisance.

I seized the opportunity with raised eyebrow to question my agreeable hostess. She nodded encouragingly in reply:

"Not out of my sight a moment since the General departed."

The secret, then, was still safe; our task to keep it so yet lay before us.

Dinner passed without incident, save that Mistress Wright, eating vast quantities of beet-root, favoured us with a discourse in support of abstaining from meat and monarchy. Only Johnson's desire to serve his King prevented him from denouncing the eccentrick American.

Dinner done, we returned to modelling in the parlour. Miss Fleay did me the honour to embark upon the task of reproducing my features; features which, she said civilly, 'twas an absolute duty to transmit to posterity, being indeed, I flatter myself, though not beautiful, yet strong and characteristick.

Mistress Wright had a mind to Dr. Johnson—"Dear creature, I must have his head"—but the Sachem was to be finished first.

The hawk face was nigh completed by bed-time, but being yet to be coloured, looked something ghostly, like a Roman busto. We left it haunting the mantelpiece as we retired. With Mistress Wright went her woman, Mr. Eden's agent, a rosy pretty-faced creature with the powerful person of a grenadier, to lie in the truckle-bed and keep the American spy under her eye till morning. Dr. Johnson carried me with him for a late stroll about the garden. On the back step sat the gardener's boy. At the locked front gate the gardener was consoling his vigil with a short pipe of tobacco. Our charge was safely surrounded till morning.

The morrow was Dr. Johnson's day at the Pottery. With more misgivings than I liked he consigned his charge to me, and stumped off towards Cheyne Walk with the gardener's boy carrying his basket behind.

I passed the day most agreeably in sensible feminine society. Much to my contentment, General B— never appeared (and I may say that through all this adventure we never laid eyes on the rakish General). Miss Fleay devoted herself assiduously to her modelling, and the moulded wax began to take on something the semblance of James Boswell. Mistress Wright had forgotten the Sachem. She took a freak to form a candle like an effigy. She fetched a roll of wax from her apartment, where Eden's agent was, finally, getting her sleep.

"Foh, how that woman sleeps!" cried Mistress Wright, little dreaming that her companion had devoted the night, not to sleep, but to surveillance.

Warming the wax by the fire, she began to pull and pinch it into the semblance of a blackamoor page. 'Twas a quaint and pretty thing, and when 'twas done at the day's end I longed to possess it. But 'twas not for me. The wax-worker wrapped it lovingly in a roll of silk, and carried it carefully off. I followed; except when retired, the lady was my charge. I found her tendering it, a folded billet, and a coin to the odd boy.

"Ma'am," said I, twitching the billet from the boy's hand, "allow *me* to be of service. I will myself take this billet in charge." I scanned the superscription: "To Joshua Fennel at the Cross Keys."

The sharp eyes measured me; the lady shrugged:

"'Tis no matter. The boy may carry the gift, and my message by word of mouth."

I gave permission with a nod.

"Say from me," Mistress Wright instructed the boy, "I desire my gift may give him light for his business."

"With permission, ma'am—" said I, and boldly unfolded the billet. 'Twas not sealed. Perusing it took but a moment. Mistress Wright desired that her gift might give him light for his business, and remained his true Christian friend.

As I scanned the missive, Dr. Sam: Johnson turned in at the gate, followed by the freckle-face potter's devil carrying the basket.

"What's to do here," says he, "and whither goes the boy?"

He indicated our messenger, now scuffing his way without hurry down Paradise Row.

"He carries a specimen of Mistress Wright's workmanship," said I, "and a message from her mouth. We have thought best to retain the written billet."

Mistress Wright smiled serenely. Dr. Johnson, scanning the billet, bellowed like a bull.

"Stop him!"

It was the freckle-face potter's lad who caught him. I was close on his heels, and had the candle out of his hand in a trice.

Mistress Wright's smile was not quite so serene; but with a fair grace she returned to the fire in the sitting-room. We left her under Miss Fleay's eye, and retired with Mistress Wright's pretty candle.

"'Tis a shame," said Dr. Johnson, regarding it, "and yet it must be done."

He shattered it. It would have cast light on the rebels' business indeed—at its core was a rolled missive:

"Pray acquaint Mr. Franklin at Passy that a new British thrust will be launched—"

"This secret is not ours," said Johnson, and to my inexpressible disappointment cast the paper into the fire.

Mistress Patience's demeanour matched her name. She conceded us the first trick, and sat serenely by the fire patting and pulling her Sachem into shape. We'd a fine dish of jugged hare to our dinner. As we relished it, Mistress Wright, eating roast potatoes, denounced us as no better than Society Islanders, that eat our fellow-creatures.

"Ma'am," says Johnson, his mouth full of hare, "you frantick republicans would upset the order and subordination of nature. And with Heaven's help, I shall myself endeavour to forfend the day."

"Thee will fail," said Mistress Wright cheerfully; "for ingenuity, he who is full of meat is no match for him who is nourisht with sallets; more especially when his cause is just."

Dr. Johnson choaked with indignation and jugged hare.

Mistress Wright carried the Sachem's head early to her chamber; her woman was at her heels. All retired betimes.

I was waked from my first light sleep by a knocking at our door. 'Twas the pretty-face grenadier, in a taking.

"Sir, she's dead. She don't breathe. Pray, pray, come to our chamber."

We struck flame to the candle, huddled on our cloathes, and ran to Mistress Wright's bed-chamber. There was the disarrayed truckle bed, as the woman had risen from it. In the shadow of the bed-curtains a figure lay motionless.

Johnson held the candle to the still face, the lappets of the night-cap falling on the high cheek-bones and sharpening the look of the nose. He touched the cold cheek. The head rolled sidewise—and kept on rolling. 'Twas severed from the trunk!

"Tschah," said Johnson, "this trick is as old as time."

He stripped back the cloathes and revealed the rolled bolster. The waxen Sachem's head fell to the ground and shattered.

"She's slipped between your fingers, woman," said he sternly to the distrest secret agent. "We must find her before she gets clear away."

"Nay, Sir, I have only nodded a moment; she cannot be far."

We ran down the stair. In the morning-room a light shewed. At Miss Fleay's writing-bureau, engaged with pen and ink, sat Mistress Wright. She had been taking refreshment, for the half of a lemon was at her elbow, and her start as we rushed in precipitated to the floor a glass half full.

"I rejoice, ma'am," said Dr. Johnson cordially, "to see that you are safe. You have given us all a turn. Pray, ma'am, allow me to escort you to your chamber."

Mistress Wright hesitated; then a second time conceded defeat. She deliberately tore into strips the written paper before her, and tossed it into the fire.

"Your most obliged, Sir," said she statelily, and laid her large well-formed hand on my friend's wrist.

The next morning the forgiving Quakeress addressed herself to the design of "having Dr. Johnson's head." She proposed to possess herself of this desirable item by means of a life mask, the secret of which she was famed to have brought to a fine art. As upon her late lamented decease her secret died with her, I will endeavour to gratify the publick by detailing her proceedings.

To begin, then, the sturdy philosopher was denuded of his upper garments and placed supine upon a couch. The application of hog's lard followed, an operation which my friend only endured with much mumbling and grumbling. He redoubled his complaints when the fair artist inserted in his nostrils two stout straws to afford him breath during the remainder of the process. Now a thin grout was swiftly plastered over his countenance, stilling his mouth and sealing his eyes in the operation. Mistress Wright worked swiftly and silently. Thinly and evenly covered with grout, the face looked ghastly as a spectre; and Mistress Wright proceeded to chill my marrow the more by swathing the corpse-like jaw with such a fold of linen as is commonly used to bind the jaws of the dead in their winding-sheets. I shuddered silently.

Dr. Johnson lay like a Stoick as succeeding layers of grout were laid on, till the mask was so thick it lost all human form.

And three minutes after the last smear was applied, all was hard and ready to remove in two neat pieces.

"Faugh," said Dr. Sam: Johnson, sitting up, red in the face and glistening with hog's lard. "'Tis too much like being buried alive; yet I rejoiced, in my prison, that my friend Boswell was by to effect my release if need arose."

"Sir," said I, acknowledging the tribute, "you may rely upon my vigilance."

"I design to do so," replied Johnson as Mistress Wright retired, "for today is my day at the pottery. Pray be more wary than last time."

Shamefacedly I promised, and pursued Mistress Wright below-stairs.

I was privileged to see Mistress Wright test her handiwork. This she did by closely pressing into the mould a thin shell of softened wax, working it into every crevice. With a kind of handle of wax she withdrew a perfect waxen mask of my revered friend's features.

"Bravo!" I cried. "The likeness is speaking! Pray, could not you gratify me with a copy?"

"Thee shall have it, James," promised the hearty Quakeress.

So saying, she summoned her woman to assist her, and disappeared with her into her own domain.

That morning saw the completion of the waxen busto of James Boswell; and I do verily believe that as fair Miss Flora's hand shaped my image in the pliable wax, so the same image was impressed upon her heart, erasing therefrom in some measure the gaudy figure of indiscreet General B——. Once I thought good to oversee the proceedings of Mistress Wright; but I found her calmly seated in her own apartment, applying the colourings of life to the waxen mask of my friend, while her woman sat stolidly by; so I returned to more congenial company.

At dinner Johnson was not by; but shortly after, I saw his familiar figure sitting in the wing chair by the fire, holding a book so close before his eyes as to brush his very eye-lashes. Mistress Wright's woman went to her dinner. It was with pleasure that I saw Mistress Wright take the opposing chair by the fire, with a cordial word that my friend, absorbed in his book, neglected to answer. I was free to walk in the garden with Miss Flora.

What was my surprize, then, as we came round the house, to see Mistress Wright, unattended, slipping down the walk with a covered basket on her arm. As I followed, I was still more thunderstruck to see Dr. Sam: Johnson approaching from the direction of Cheyne Walk. He met her as she left the gate.

"Well met, Mistress Wright. Allow me to relieve you of your burden. Whither do we carry it?"

Her countenance changed no more than the waxen Sachem's which it resembled.

"To the pottery, friend Samuel."

He bowed and handed her with courtly mien. I was glad to make one in the expedition, having been a prisoner in the house since our vigil started.

I shuddered as we passed Dr. Driffield's private mad-house, euphemistically denominated "the Academy". We turned into Lawrence Street, passed the sign of the Cross Keys, and came to the Chelsea China Manufactory.

The potters looked their surprise at seeing Dr. Sam: Johnson so precipitately returned; but among the mixing-rooms he had a cubicle of his own, and thither we turned our steps. The fire still burned on the hearth to give us warmth. Mistress Wright set down her basket, which Dr. Johnson officiously undertook to turn out. 'Twas filled with rumpled old gazettes.

Dr. Johnson carefully uncovered the white unblemished wasp's-nest shape, and set it to one side, scanning each gazette with care. Though he could detect no scribbled word, he prudently consigned all to the flames. Now for the first time I saw Mistress Wright's Red-Indian composure broken. She snatched ineffectually at his hand; the tears started in her eyes as the flames took the gazettes, and we saw the brown spidery writing start up with the heat.

"I thought so," said Dr. Sam: Johnson with satisfaction. "Lemonade indeed! You have been writing with it, ma'am, not quaffing it; and I counsel you to turn your attention to good roast meat, if you expect to prevail at this game."

"I will do so," said the angry rebel between her teeth, "and I will prevail."

I heard with satisfaction the instructions issued to the freckle-face boy for preserving the mould that should gratify me with a busto of my illustrious friend; and then we walked back towards Paradise Row in the falling twilight.

At home a new wonder awaited me. I entered the drawing-room with my illustrious friend, in his snuff-colour suit and second-best wig; and there, in second-best brown suit and best wig, holding the book to his eyes, he sat in the wing chair by the fire! I looked from the Johnson at my elbow to the Johnson by the fire, and realized how I had been duped by the wily rebel and her wax-works. But for my wilier friend, I had permitted to happen the catastrophe we sought to avoid!

Sternly admonished, the waiting-woman sat up through the night, and Mistress Wright was for the nonce muzzled. On the morrow, it seemed, she took Dr. Johnson's advice; for when Mistress Wright joined us at table for the mid-day meal, her woman whispered me that she had spent the morning dressing a roast duck!

"So, ma'am," I rallied the lady, "you have become converted to our way of thinking, and have drest a succulent roast duck, which no doubt we are now about to sample."

"No, sir," replied she readily, though I thought she looked put about, "for nothing less than sweet charity would I require a fellow-creature to give up its life. 'Tis for a poor man, lies ill at the Cross Keys."

"I applaud your benevolence, ma'am," says Johnson, "and desire to imitate it. Come, let us all go down to the Cross Keys."

Accordingly the duck was fetched in its basket, covered by a linen napkin.

"Ma'am," says Johnson, peeking and sniffing the tempting aroma, "pray tell me, how have you stuft this tender fellow-creature?"

He probed at the filled cavity with his finger, and tasted the fragrant stuffing.

"This is too bad of thee, Samuel!" cried charitable Mistress Wright. "Think of the poor man!"

"He'll not grudge me a bite," says Johnson coolly, and pulled out a handful of dressing. Something came with it—a billet, folded small and tied with packthread. Johnson's smile became broad.

"Fie!" he cried. "How came this waste paper to mar such a dish!"

He tossed it in the fire, where it spluttered and flared to nothing in an odour of burning grease. Mistress Wright turned on her heel and left the roast duck to an inevitable fate.

There was no poor man ill at the Cross Keys, so much we learned of Eden's agents; neither had Joshua Fennel ever been heard of. Dr. Sam: Johnson muttered to himself upon this intelligence, and resolved to go no more to the Pottery until the matter was safely concluded. It fell to my lot to carry his commissions to the potters.

"At Dr. Johnson's service, Mr. Boswell," said the master potter, "and pray say to him, we deeply regret the accidental destruction of his mould, and desire he'll soon commission another—"

"Destruction!" I cried. "Is the mould destroyed, and no copy taken off?"

"Aye, with a pox on Josh and his clumsy fingers."

"He deserves," I cried, "to be soundly swinged."

"And swinged he shall be, when once I can lay my hands on him. Pray say so to Dr. Johnson."

Upon receipt of this bad news, Mistress Wright was eager to set about making a new mould; but Dr. Sam: Johnson incontinently refused.

"No, ma'am; you'll stop up my eyes no more."

Mistress Wright thereupon sulked; she sat with folded hands, and would not partake of the convivial punch which Miss Fleay that night brewed. Casting off care in the presence of my penetrating friend, I sped the hours in gallant drinking of healths; Miss Fleay and I were merry together; I felt the shadow of General B—totally withdrawn, and longed to take his place with the lady that night. But, foxed though I was, duty restrained me; I left Miss Fleay to the punch, and Mistress Wright to the care of her woman, and followed my respected friend to our chamber.

He scowled upon me; I felt an uneasy sense of having exceeded prudence. I slumped on the bed.

"Resume your coat, sir," said he, "and stand up, if you can. I am uneasy for the safety of our secret, and mean to keep watch to-night."

We tiptoed down the stair and took up our stand in the garden under the American's window. A light shewed, and two figures moved in the room. The curtains were drawn; in a little the light was extinguished. Then nothing, only darkness. A great drowse fell upon me. I cannot say how long I floated in it, but I know I was brought back with the jerk of a thumb in my ribs. Down the vine that rose to the window was clambering the figure of a man.

We closed in upon the spot where the intruder must take to the ground; when with a savage leap the dark figure hurled itself down from above our heads, dashed us momentarily to the ground, and made off towards the stables.

In a trice Johnson had recovered himself, pulled me to my feet, and reached the stable door in time to see the man leap to the bare back of Miss Fleay's own horse and ride out at the opened door. There was nothing to do but follow suit. Johnson must have got the General's horse—I marvelled at the agility with which he kept his seat on the mettlesome creature, holding to the halter with one hand. I followed riding loose and reckless on a less fleet creature.

There was no sound in Paradise Row save the sound of galloping hoofs. For the moment the stranger had the start of us. Then we began to gain. At the corner of Cheyne Walk the rider ahead passed under the street-lamp, and we saw the hawk-like profile and the piercing eyes—'twas the Quakeress herself in male attire! Though she rode with reckless skill, we were still gaining as we gallopped in a string up Cheyne Walk. There were lights in the private mad-house; I shuddered to think of the wretches incarcerated there.

"This is too dangerous," shouted Johnson over his shoulder. "If we cannot confine the frantick rebel one way, we must try another."

Before I could divine his meaning he had flung his pocket knife boldly through the closed window of Driffield's Academy. It brought the attendants to the gates in a trice; they were after us, hallooed on by Johnson, as we overhauled our quarry at the foot of Cheyne Row.

Johnson pulled down the horse she was riding. She sat erect and impassive as the mad-house attendants came level with us. Then the boldness of Johnson's scheam, so suddenly formed in his mind, became apparent.

"Alack, gentlemen," his Lichfield burr was suddenly strong, "I fear we have arouzed you late. This frantick wife of mine—" Patience Wright suddenly looked full at him with startled gaze—"this frantick poor creature should have been consigned to your care at a more reasonable hour, but that she suddenly gave us the slip at the ordinary and escaped in my attire as you see—"

I looked at her garb. It was indeed Dr. Johnson's second-best brown.

"Pray conduct us to Dr. Driffield."

I saw defeat in the American's eye; but I reckoned without her bold slyness. Narrowly watched by the attendants, and with one of us on each side, she was conducted through the portals of the mad-house, and the heavy door swung to behind us. Dr. Driffield received us, rubbing his fat hands.

"Hark ye, Doctor," said Mistress Wright, cool and collected, "a word in your ear. I am your debtor for delivering me, for yonder husband of mine—" impudently indicating Johnson—"is mad as the wind, and a sly madman he is. Coming hither to consign him to your care, he found means at the ordinary to deprive me of my attire and confine me. I gave him the slip in a suit of his cloathes, but he was nigh catching me, and it had gone hard with me but for a fortunate chance—in a fit of madness he flung a missile through your window, and so it chanced that your keepers have laid him by the heels. I beg you'll not credit his sly lies; for yonder lies his missile—" she nodded to it where it lay on the floor—"and the better to assure you he's mad indeed, he imagines himself in his phrenzy to be one of London's most famous men."

Johnson was indeed inflating himself to thunder out a denial of this impudent fabrication.

"Sir," he began, "I am Samuel Johnson—"

"Is it likely?" counters this impudent American. "Has Sam: Johnson a wife? Nay, is Sam: Johnson in London? You know from the gazettes he is gone to Oxford."

Dr. Driffield, alas, proved to be a great reader of the gazettes. "True, ma'am," says he.

"I am Sam: Johnson," said my friend calmly, "and there are weighty reasons of state why this mad-woman must be confined."

"Be perswaded, sir," I cried, "this is indeed the Great Lexicographer, and I am James Boswell, at your service."

Unfortunately our midnight dash had discommoded my vitals. I hiccupped. Mistress Wright turned to me with scorn.

"What, Thomas!" she cried. "Is this the part of one who has been in my service, man and boy, for fourteen years! Take care, sirrah, you'll lose my favour. You have been bought by this old reprobate, 'tis clear—"

The hiccup did my business. Dr. Driffield used his own nose, and put me down for the drunken serving-man she made me seem.

"Away with them, men," says he.

"I'll not stir till this woman is confined," cried Johnson stoutly.

The fat doctor looked on him sourly. The American woman might have got clear off, had she but let well enough alone. But when one of the hulking mad-keepers laid a doubtful hand on her arm, she lost her head.

"Touch me," she cried defiantly, "at your peril; the Queen is my friend."

"You see," said Johnson to the mad-doctor, "her brain is addled."

Driffield looked from one to the other of us in perplexity.

"They're all mad," he decided. "Let them be confined."

I stared aghast as my revered friend was seized; while Johnson held the American spy in a grip of iron. Clearly so long as she was confined he had no care for us.

For four-and-twenty hours I saw my friend no more. Dawn came on, and with it thoughts as painful as the head they filled.

The sun was high when one of the mad-keepers gingerly thrust some hard bread and a bowl of water between the bars.

The hours dragged on. As my head cleared from the fumes of the punch, I began to feel a savage hunger. I would gladly have devoured Mistress Wright's roast duck, secret writings and all, if I could have come by it. The thought of the duck recalled to me the task we had set ourselves, and I rejoiced that even at this cost we had found a way to confine the frantick rebel with her secret still undivulged. Let her remain under restraint until the moment of danger should be past.

Nevertheless, I had scarce resigned myself to a like fate for myself and my friend. As my head cleared, I resolved to strike a stroke for freedom. When the burly mad-keeper returned at sun-down, I was ready for him.

"What say you," said I perswasively through the bars, "to a handful of broad pieces?"

I saw in his eye that the mad-keeper could be bought; but he was wary.

"You've never a handful of broad pieces about you," he muttered, measuring my garb.

"True for you," said I; "but hark'ee, friend, my master has a purse of golden guineas in the keeping of the landlord of the Cross Keys; how if I was to come to him and say, my master sent for 'em? We should have the dividing of 'em between us."

"Done," said the mad-keeper instantly, and added slyly: "We'll go together."

I could hope for no better. The mad-keeper instantly set me free, and led the way through a tangle of outbuildings towards Lawrence Street and the Cross Keys. I kept ever alert to give my conductor the slip; but he pressed along with his arm linked in mine, and I was a prisoner still. Before the Cross Keys we halted.

"We must not enter together," said I with firmness. "The landlord will scarce yield the bag of guineas if I come with an accomplice at my elbow. Do you go in and bespeak a pot; I'll follow, get the swag, and join you as if by chance."

"Ye'll make off, ye mean," rasped the mad-keeper with a cunning look. "No, no, me lad; *you* go in, and I'll follow. And look ye don't get out of my sight."

I shrugged, and went in.

"Hark'ee, landlord," I began to speak quietly and hastily to the thin needle-nose little man at the bar. But for him the smoky dark-panelled room was empty. He looked at me with disfavour. I saw in his eyes as in a mirror how I must look, rumpled, pasty-faced from punch and lack of sleep, and my heart sank. Over his shoulder I saw the door open, and in came the mad-keeper. He grinned evilly at me, and took up a post of vigilance on the settle by the fire.

The landlord listened to my muttered plea without change of expression, and then shook his head. He absolutely refused to send a messenger all the way to Whitehall. He seemed apprehensive that I was the advance guard of the running smobble.

"Then pray, landlord," I shifted my ground, "pray let the pot-boy be sent no further than Miss Fleay's in Paradise Row, I'll engage he'll be well paid for his trouble."

The landlord continued to look at me, impassive.

"The lady affects me," I lied desperately. " 'Tis an *affaire du coeur*, 'pon honour, landlord, do but befriend me, you'll be well rewarded, pray let me have ink and paper and the pot-boy to carry my billet."

The sharp little face suddenly split in a wide smile. There was not a tooth in the grinning gums.

"Faith, lad, if 'tis the heart is in it, I'll befriend thee," lisped he, "being myself a great sufferer from the tender passion."

He set paper and pen before me. As I dipped the quill, he set himself with relish to peer over my shoulder and enjoy the composition of my *billet doux*. I ground my teeth, and wrote:

"Honour'd Madam:

He who loves you better than life, acquaints you that our time is ripe, for my schoolmaster Mr. J. is detained in Cheyne Walk, at the Academy, whence he will scarce come off with ease. Pray be circumspect, for should Eden hear of this he would enlarge him instanter. You take my meaning. I am detained at the Cross Keys by a bailiff—[The landlord glanced at my mad-keeper, and then back to me, and shook his head commiseratingly, as if to communicate the sympathy of a fellow-sufferer equally from bailiffs and the tender passion]—but I will take what means I may to give him the slip and come to you, whereby we may have the consolation of one another's company.

Thine till death,

J.B."

The pot-boy was rouzed from the kitchen ingle-nook, and off he went for Paradise Row. I returned willy-nilly to my mad-keeper, and told him the first tale that came to my head, that mine host had sent for the keys, and the guineas should shortly be ours. The man scowled into his pot.

Now up comes mine host, and with a wink to me, sets out to ply the sullen mad-keeper with liquor, lacing his pots with gin with the liberal hand of a friend to lovers. Four pots later the boy returned with a verbal message: "The lady bids me say, she takes your meaning, and will deal with your schoolmaster." The mad-keeper was too owlishly drunk to do more than blink foolishly. A few moments more, and his head dropped to the table. With a broad grin full of gums the landlord jerked his head in signal, and I was off in a trice. I came into Cheyne Walk just as Sir William Eden descended from his carriage at the mad-doctor's door. Soon my learned friend was once more at liberty, no whit the worse for his Academic sojourn, he having born it as a philosopher.

That day week, all danger past, we were once more at Dr. Drif-field's door, and the frantick American, still wearing Dr. Johnson's second-best brown, was in her turn enlarged.

"No hard feelings, ma'am," said Dr. Johnson; "we have gained time, and time fights for the King."

"I'll kiss thee farewell," replied Mistress Wright, smiling, "in token of Christian forgiveness."

Dr. Johnson, magnanimous in victory, bore her Christian salute with a good grace.

We saw no more of the American wax-worker; but as Christmas came on we had a message from her.

"I am to say from the lady," said the messenger, "she desires it may cast light upon your business."

We stared upon the message, a slab of such petrified grout as had formed the ill-fated life-mask of the Great Lexicographer.

"This is an Egyptian message," puzzled I as the messenger with-drew. "I can make nothing of this."

"It comes with the candle-message," mused Johnson. "We shat-tered the candle; are we to shatter this as well?"

Boswell: "Will it shatter like wax?"

Johnson: "The mould was shattered. The mould . . . Stay, Mr. Boswell, you oversaw its making, pray detail to me the manner of it."

Boswell: "Well, sir, she smeared your face with grout, and braced it with a fold of linen—"

Johnson: "A fold of linen! Why did I not hear of this?"

Boswell: "Nay, sir, you were by."

Johnson: "I was by! Deafened and blinded with grout! *'Twas the message!*"

BOSWELL: "Nay, sir, the linen was blank."

JOHNSON: "Blank! Tschah! 'Twas writ in secret ink. The Americans have had the secret after all!"

Angrily he dashed the slab to the hearth. It shattered. Folded within lay a strip of linen protecting a slip of paper. The paper was from that day's gazette:

"We are advized from New-York, that Lieutenant-general John Burgoyne—"

"Of course," remarked Johnson, "Gentleman Johnny Burgoyne. Who else would take a lady of Drury Lane into keeping while great events depended?"

"—Lieutenant-general John Burgoyne with 6,000 men has surrendered to the rebels near Saratoga in the Province of New-York. This stroke has much heartened the rebels, and 'tis thought that his Majesty the King of France will now conclude an alliance . . ."

Johnson threw down the item in disgust, and picked up the linen. Written on it in a curiously rusty-looking stuff was a letter from the American spy:

"Sir,

Pray accept of my acknowledgements for the help Dr. Johnson lately rendered the glorious cause of Liberty, in transporting with his own hand, the mould which carried that most necessary communication to Mr. Franklin, into the hands of my accomplice the potter's boy. The comedy of the mad-house served to keep the minions of the King amused until the boy had made the best of his way out of the country. How well he did his part, this glorious victory of Saratoga attests. With the blessings of a great and grateful nation, I am,

Sir,

Your oblig'd humble servant,

PATIENCE WRIGHT"

[By growling against the rebellious Colonists, the Great Cham invited at my hands this fictitious come-uppance dealt him by a factual American spy. The Chelsea scene suggested the China Manufactory, which Johnson frequented, and the mad "Academy," which he did not.]

SAINT-GERMAIN THE DEATHLESS

(*London, 1770*)

Saint-Germain the Deathless, that mysterious being, was heralded in the gay world of London by a gipsy's prophecy, and given his congée by Dr. Sam: Johnson, detector of chicane; in both which events I, James Boswell of Auchinleck, played my part. But of the wizard's advent we had as yet no premonition when upon an autumn night in the year 1770 I carried my philosophical friend to see Mrs. Cornelys' Venetian ridotto in Soho; unless indeed my companion's strictures on the ridotto were premonitory:

"A publick ridotto," declared he roundly, "is the prologue to publick mischiefs innumerable, as, wenching, gaming, coney-catching, the *prig* and the *snatch*—"

To this proposition I did not assent, though in the light of future events I ought to have done. Instead I remarked:

"If this is so, sir, I wonder that you give yourself the fatigue of coming hither, the more especially as you will not masque."

Amid Mrs. Cornelys' Chinese silks and lacquers, that multiplied in her hundred mirrors and threw back the sparkle of her thousand candles, the sturdy philosopher stood four-square, uncompromisingly himself in snuff-coloured broadcloth, complaisant good humour twinkling in his large light-grey eyes and playing over his strong, pock-scarred visage. To my remark he replied merely:

"Look about you, Bozzy, and wonder no longer." I looked upon the motley rout of masquers, sailing past us, round and round, to the sounding of fiddles and flutes. "Here is man in microcosm; and man is ever my study."

"Man?" I was laughing at the absurd anticks of a Pegasus whose wildly flapping mechanical wings could neither get it off the ground nor impel its two tangled pairs of legs smoothly in the same direction.

"Why, sir, man in disguise is man most revealed."

"How do you make that good?"

"Consider. At the ridotto man escapes himself, to become what he would rather be. Behold James Boswell, Esq:, advocate.—" I regarded myself in the long mirror. 'Twas true, I wished the long nose shorter, the swarthy skin ruddy, the stature higher by six inches. Nonetheless, I thought it a gallant enough figure I saw reflected, decked out in ruby velvet riding-coat and snow-white buckskins. Dr. Sam: Johnson thought otherwise.

"You are tired of the law. Hither you come, personating, in your conceit, a more romantick figure—the Gentleman Highwayman."

"Yet I trust, sir, that I am more Gentleman than Highwayman."

"What do you say, then, to yonder fellow who yearns to return to the Garden of Eden? And what an Eve he has chosen!"

Adam's pink silk sheath was so all-revealing it made the ladies blush and stare. His Eve had chosen to appear in the briefest of bodices, the gauziest of petticoats, the tallest of powdered wigs, and the most diamonds. She sailed along superbly, high-bosomed, long-limbed, rolling bold blue eyes left and right behind her masque of lace and velvet.

"Nay, Bozzy, you perceive here's another use for the ridotto, the publick exposure of one's wares."

"Not so, sir, there you are out; this lady is not for sale. This is Miss Fanny Hall."

"Oh, then she is sold already."

It was too true, as all the world well knew. Her ripe beauties she had long since brought to market, and made a good bargain. She was the acknowledged inamorata of the sardonic sea-faring Earl of F——. It was he who had loaded her white wrists and whiter throat with the diamonds that so ill suited with Paradisal simplicity. Tonight she was wearing the famous Brouwere necklace, a replica of that made by the same jeweller for the Empress of Russia. The necklace, they say, was her price, and the jeweller executed it in the Golconda diamonds the Earl had fetched from India. As the malicious whisper ran, the Earl had had her at cut rate after all, for the Empress' stones outweighed hers two to one; but Mistress Fan, never having seen the Empress or her necklace, flaunted the Earl's gift in ignorant bliss.

As to the Earl, he was now at sea with the Fleet; but Mistress Fanny was showing no signs of being inconsolable. Masquers dangled after: a devil in red, a grasshopper in green, a medley of dominos. Let them dangle; I had a scheam to scatter them. What an adventure for me, were I to win my way over so many rivals, not by diamonds, but by my single power of address! Surely James Boswell, young, amorous, and quick of wit, could distance the field and hornify the Earl . . .

My friend's sonorous voice shattered my candle-light dreams: "And behold this superannuated houri, such as the bravest Musselman might quake to meet in Paradise. How much more seemly is the flowing crimson domino that follows." The crimson domino tipped me a most unseemly wink.

"And what is this siege-engine in purple velvet?"

'Twas Mrs. Cornelys herself, a formidable Juno, her once handsome visage as seamy as her rumored past. She stood forth, stilled the fiddles and bade the merrymakers unmask.

"Now masques are dropped," my friend moralized on, "and fancy gives way to reality, action ensues upon desire. The houri will carry her partner to Paradise, Adam will have his Eve—"

"He may not, sir," said I, adding inwardly: *"For I hope I shall have her."*

"He may so, sir; nay, Pegasus may fly. Yet if you find yourself in Bow Street, Bozzy, for going on the heath to cry 'Stand and deliver!' send not to me to go your bail!"

A hand tugged my sleeve. 'Twas the little red domino.

"Come quick, Mr. Boswell, for the gipsy is about to read Miss Fanny's fortune!"

"What, cartomancy is toward?" cried Dr. Johnson. "The coneycatching commences! I'll none of it!"

I smiled. That 'twas coney-catching indeed, none knew better than I. I had already (to confess all in a word) concerted my scheam with Mrs. Cornelys' gipsy soothsayer, telling her what to say and feeing her well to say it. Miss Fanny was greedy for marvels. Let a soothsayer but put me forward, and my affair must prosper. But of this I said nothing.

"What, sir," I protested politely, "will you so soon be gone?"

"I'm for bed betimes. I must be in Streatham tomorrow, and Mrs. Thrale brooks no delay."

"Streatham indeed," said I sourly, for I grudged the volatile lady her half-weekly share of my learned friend's company. "At Streatham you'll find as much masquing and mumming as shall last you a month."

"But no cartomancy," said Dr. Johnson sternly. He gave me a curt nod, and made off.

In the Chinese supper-room the Romany seeress awaited only the presence of her claudestine employer—myself. Her beady eye caught mine, and the ceremony began. Curious faces ringed the table as the wrinkled old gipsy laid out the Tarot pack, the mysterious Egyptian cards that figure the future.

Mistress Fan hung over the strange pictured cards. In the centre was set out a woman meshed in a whirlwind—"Yourself, pretty lady."

"And see, round about a crowd of men," cried Miss Fanny, preening. "Here's one wears a broad hat, a mountebank, by his seeming—"

"The Juggler—trust him not, milady."

"And here's one—how frightsome!—leads a spotted beast. A hyena?"

"The Alchemist—avoid him, milady."

I plucked at the gaudy sleeve. These cards were nothing to my purpose. A better card fell at once.

"What shall signify this booted rider of swarthy mien? See, he carries a great disc of gold!" Mistress Fanny's pink tongue touched her pouting lip.

"The Knight of Coins, the Tartar Knight, milady—a dark man, a lover, he brings money in his hand, and much money around him—see the cards, the nine golden sequins, the eight guineas of gold, the ten crowns—the dark lover brings much money, madam."

"O brave dark man!" cried the courtesan, who as all the world knew was as greedy for gold as for marvels.

"Why, Fan, sure 'tis Mr. Boswell!" cried my little friend in the red domino, innocently forwarding my scheam, "for see, he's dark as any Spaniard!"

My swarthy countenance in the mirror smiled back at me.

"Poh!" struck in a new voice huskily. "This dark man is never young Boswell. Where should a Scotch lairdie come by so much coin?"

I scowled upon the speaker. 'Twas that plaguy old harridan, Mrs. Cornelys.

"Much money? Nay," she proclaimed, "I can tell you who this dark man will be—and see yonder where he stands!"

Every eye followed her gesture. In the doorway towered a new masquer, one who supported the character of an astrologer. His long black robe glittered with diamond stars. His pointed mage's steeple brushed the lintel above his head. In his long-nosed Venetian masque he loomed like some frightsome genie of legend.

"Pray, Mrs. Cornelys, what is he?"

I thought the woman gave me a malicious smile as she answered Mistress Fan's question:

"A foreign nobleman of great wealth, come to London incognito."

"If he comes incognito," muttered I sourly, "then how do you know him?"

"He cannot deceive me, for I knew him in old days at Amsterdam. What his right name is, no man knows; but he is called Saint-Germain the Deathless."

"How, deathless?"

"They say he will never die. Some people think he is the Wandering Jew, and has been on this earth since Christ at His passion bade him tarry. Nor does he deny it. Sometimes he lets slip a word, as if he remembered times long out of memory, of Pontius Pilate and of Tamas Kouli-Khan."

"What does he live on?"

"On a magical elixir, they say, which he brews himself, being an adept and an alchemist, and this gives him eternal youth."

As if on cue, the tall alchemist in the doorway drew off the masque, revealing a dark hawk's face with glittering black eyes lighting such features as an ancient statue in bronze might bear.

"He lives on air, say others," Mrs. Cornelys gabbled glibly on, "being a sylph or elemental."

"Poh," said Miss Fanny impatiently, "I care not for his diet, I. What estate has he? What money, eh?"

"A great estate, though no man knows surely where it lies. He is plentifully supplied with precious stones. The ones you see upon his robe are the least of his treasure. Some say that in his wanderings he has discovered the secret of the diamond mines of Golconda."

The grasshopper, now revealed as little Minick the jeweller, stared upon the wizard and sucked his lip.

"Others say," continued Mrs. Cornelys with relish, "that he has discovered the Philosopher's Stone, and makes diamonds. One day, so the story runs, falling in converse with the French King about gems, and inspecting a goodly diamond, Saint-Germain offered by his art to double it in size. Taking it, he returned to the King next day a great flawless gem of the first water, for which the King's lapidary offered ten thousand louis on the spot."

"Ten thousand louis!" Mistress Fanny swept aside the Tarot cards and rose with decision. "Fetch him hither!"

So fast do the best-laid scheams of mortal man, in our old Scots phrase, gang agley! There stood I forgotten, while Mistress Fan held out her white hand to the lips of Saint-Germain the Deathless!

"Monsieur le Comte," cooed Mistress Fan, "is it true that you are a wizard?"

To this had all my hopes and scheams fallen! Within the Chinese alcove, tête-à-tête, Mistress Fanny Hall and Saint-Germain the Deathless sipped sillabub. From the large supper room glasses clinked; in the salon a harpsichord tinkled. Scorning dance and refreshment alike, I stood glowering, unseen, muffled in someone's discarded domino, intent only to watch over Mistress Fan, for the wizard disquieted me. As a gentleman, I stopped my ears; but such a turning did their discourse take, that I soon unstopped them again.

"Is it true, as they say, that you can make diamonds?"

The black brows lifted.

"Alas, no, Madame. There is no person who can make diamonds, without he have diamonds to begin."

His speech was fluent, his tone deep and soothing. The faint accent eluded me. Was it French or Italian, Dutch or High Dutch? Or was it in truth the accent of that dark street in Jerusalem two thousand years ago? I could not tell. It had some smack of all, with a mellow deep-throated tune that was the man's own.

"But if you have diamonds," persisted the Earl's mistress in her silver voice. "If you have diamonds? They say you doubled a great diamond for the French King."

"I may have done."

"Then you shall shew me how you do it."

"Ah, no, milady, such doings are not for you to see. It would affright the strongest, and there is desperate danger, if the pentagram fail. But come, give me your necklace, eh, I'll return it doubled."

"Doubled!" The greedy eyes were sparkling. I scowled. "'Twill be beyond compare in the world!"

She put her hand to the clasp, and paused.

"But stay, how do I know you'll return it?—Nay, never bridle and scowl. You shall augment it while I am by."

"'Twill be the harder," shrugged the wizard, "but I'll essay it."

Again her hand paused.

"How do I know you can do what you claim? How do I know my diamonds will not dissolve and puff to dust under your hand?"

"You do not know," said the wizard angrily. His sombre height towered over her. "I do not seek this task, milady. If you distrust me, I'll e'en bid you good night."

"Poh," laughed Miss Fan. "Sit down again. You shall augment me but one little diamond, to shew your art."

"You will blab it, and I shall be beset by all the greedy and curious of London."

"Trust me, not I."

"You will not be afraid?"

"Not with you." Blue eyes smiled into brown, a soft white hand touched long dark fingers, and the wizard yielded to the charm.

"Then I will do it. First, your diamond."

The courtesan widened her eyes at him.

"*My* diamond? Will you not augment me one of yours?"

"They are augmented already. The diamond, you comprehend, is of a density. If you understand his nature, you may stretch him until he become as two. Then beware! If you force him yet, on the instant, pouf! he will explode to dust, and you no longer have the diamond. No, no, madame; I must practise upon a virgin gem."

Mistress Fan, as all the world knew, was kept by the Earl well provided in diamonds. "You shall have one," she assented.

"And let it be of moderate size, milady."

"Why?"

"Because I say so. It is I who risk my life within the pentagram."

"Risk life?"

In the candlelight the mage's intense dark eyes sparkled wildly.

"These are deep secrets to which I admit you," he said in his vibrant voice. "Some of this lore I had of Friar Bacon in England some hundreds of years ago. On some points it fell to Theophrastus Paracelsus in the Cinquecento to set me right. Some details I am still to perfect. Therein lies the danger."

"How so?"

"Know, madame, the secret: In all things resideth the same primal matter, *materia prima;* to the which is superadded of the four elements, earth, air, fire, and water, so much of each as may vary the properties of things."

Unseen without the alcove, I listened ensorcelled, half vigilant to watch over my lady, half in superstitious awe.

"Your diamond, milady," the voice went on, "though he come out of the earth and have a gleam of the water, yet in his perfection is he most tinct with fire. Now in each element resideth a spirit, an elemental by name, in air, the sylph, in earth, the elf, in water, the undine, and in fire, the salamander. These elementals are spirits very wilful and powerful; a man might better tame wild horses, if he were not sure of his powers. A strong and fearless man by compelling their aid may so rend apart, as it were, the very being of the diamond, that he may expand it from within to the very limits of its boundaries. Do you understand me?"

I doubted it; but Miss Fan nodded with wide eyes.

"I control these wild spirits by threads of gossamer," said the alchemist solemnly. "If they break loose, they will rend us both. Therefore, whatever you may see or hear, you must make no noise nor move a muscle—no, not though you see the heavens falling and the ground opening and flood and flame bursting forth, for once the pentacle is drawn you have no hope save in me."

"And what of you?"

"I am Saint-Germain the Deathless. Me they will assail in vain. I will protect you, if you obey me."

"I will obey you," said Mistress Fan in a very small voice.

"Then let us set about it." The magician rose, his velvet robe billowing about him. Hastily I shrank into the adjacent alcove, amid a litter of walnut shells and purple splashes of claret.

"Conduct me," commanded the wizard, "to your lodging."

"To my lodging!" The slut made herself look sanctimoniously horrified.

"I shall require a space suitable to my purpose," said the alchemist coldly, "having fire on the hearth and water nearby. Earth and air I'll make shift to supply."

"But at midnight?" breathed Miss Fanny.

"'Tis the most prosperous hour. Come, let us go."

There went my hopes for the night, past recall! The rooms were emptying. The gipsy crone was gone to her tents; but the Tarot pack still littered her deserted table. I scowled upon the scattered cards. The Tartar Knight rode on with a silly smirk. The ugly Alchemist leered sidewise at me. I tore the leer in two and left the pieces on the table. I longed to do the like to Saint-Germain the Deathless.

"Well, Bozzy, what news?"

Thus was I greeted, three days later, by my philosophick friend, new-returned from Streatham. He sat much at his ease in his pleasant parlour in Johnson's Court. The emptied tea pot was pushed aside, the ample snuff-coloured waistcoat was unbuttoned, and social cordiality reigned upon his cragged countenance.

"Wonders, sir, wonders! You recall the ridotto? Well, sir, next day when I waited at Miss Fanny Hall's levee—

"Give me leave to say, Bozzy, this ardour to wait upon another man's doxy does you scant credit."

"Nay, sir, there's more to it than gallantry. What do you say to the Philosopher's Stone?"

"What do you call the Philosopher's Stone? The art by which Miss Fanny Hall coins men's hearts is older than the alchemist's."

"The alchemist, that's my theme. What do you say to a wizard that doubles the size of diamonds?"

"I say humbug, sir."

"Nay, Dr. Johnson, hear me out."

He did so, in smiling complaisance tinged with derision.

"And trust me, sir," I completed the tale, "she had it out of the fire doubled, blue-white, of the first water, exquisitely cut. Do not scoff, sir, for I quote old Minick the jeweller. Miss Fan had it under his eye in the morning, and these are his words."

"Well, well, little Minick will not lie. This alchemist has a secret to conjure with. Pray, Bozzy, did not you contrive to make one at the conjuration, that you may also make your fortune?"

"Alas, no, sir, 'twas a conjuration à deux."

"Nor did you not question the lady as to what passed?"

"Be sure that I did, sir, it being a subject most curious, on the which I would gladly be enlightened. But Mistress Fan turns pale at the thought, and all I can learn is this: that there was a dazzle of red wildfire, and a reek as of the Pit, and then the demons rapt away her senses and left her in a swound; from which recovering, there was the augmented diamond in her hand. What do you say, is he not a wizard, this Saint-Germain the Deathless?"

"Saint-Germain! Oh ho, now I see the light. I remember the Comte de Saint-Germain, in the days when he lived at London and intrigued for the Stuart Pretender. Stay, here is a bit of trash that concerns him."

Dr. Johnson rooted a moment among tall folios on his dusty book shelf, and handed me a vilely printed broadsheet bearing an inky woodcut and lines of doggerel.

Like all such things, the wretched engraving bore little resemblance to the man himself as he had appeared at the ridotto. The graver had given the pointed face a sardonic lift of the brow, a sly quirk of the lip, that seemed to laugh at the solemn character the rhymester had given to the wizard in the doggerel blackly printed underneath:

LE COMTE DE SAINT-
GERMAIN
CELEBRATED ALCHEMIST

Even as Prometheus, he stole the Fire
By which the World exists, and all Men respire,
Nature at his Voice must lay down her Lyre,
If he is not a god himself, a God does him inspire.

"There he is, to the life," said Dr. Johnson with a smile. "Many a night has he sat by my fireside and discoursed of strange marvels. A singular being he is, and of a quizzing humour; but he is not therefore immortal. It is singular enough behaviour if he chooses thus to make a lady a secret gift from his store of gems; but he is not thereby an alchemist. More likely a prestidigitator. Had he been searched when his hocus-pocus was done, the smaller diamond would have been found hid about his person."

"Nay, sir, do not deprive me of my faith in the Philosopher's Stone."

"Well, well, Bozzy, I should soon hear the straight of it did I but know where my old friend lodges. I must put him on his guard against the harpy Hall."

"What, you have been rusticated indeed. Have you not seen your *Publick Advertiser?*"

I unfolded it where it lay neglected, and read out:

"M. Le Comte de Saint-Germain, called 'Trompe-le-Mort' (which is to say Diddle-Death), is newly come to London, and lodges at the Cross Keys. In the drawing-rooms of Mayfair he bears away the bell, and rumour will have it, that he will meet with a certain *lady of the town,* at a certain *witching hour,* to display his *marvels* to her, in conjuring of diamonds or otherhow. What marvels the lady will requite him with, is beyond our province to inquire."

Johnson: "Come, this is brazen. What will the Earl say?"

Boswell: "He has said it. The Fleet is in port. He walks in upon us hard upon the heels of the lapidary, and Miss Fan, afire as she is—"

Johnson: "For Saint-Germain?"

Boswell: "For diamonds. Miss Fan could scarce support the interval; but by great good fortune, the Earl has business in the country, Miss Fan is left to her own devices, and tonight comes the great conjury."

Johnson: "What, he will conjure again?"

Boswell: "Aye, sir, now that he has proved his mastery Mistress Fanny is in haste to have her great necklace augmented."

Johnson: "Sure he'll never undertake it. This would cost him too dear in diamonds."

Boswell: "He has undertaken it."

Johnson: "What, another conjury à deux?"

Boswell: "No, sir. He has frighted Miss Fan with his wildfire, and she will have a protector by her side—James Boswell, at her service."

I smirked the satisfaction I felt.

Johnson: "And *quis custodiet ipsos custodes,* Who shall guard the guard? I said it, there's coney-catching toward, and I fear the gentlemen, my friends, are the coneys."

He clapped his little three-cornered hat on his old brown scratch-wig.

Johnson: "I'll e'en pay my old friend a call at the Cross Keys."

As twilight fell, I was before The Turk's Head inhaling the scent of roasting buttock of beef, when Dr. Sam: Johnson came along the foot-way, touching each post as he passed, and muttering to himself.

"Well, sir, did you see your old friend at the Cross Keys?"

"Yes, sir, I saw him, and I shall make one at the conjury, at his express invitation, nay at his insistence. Will you not dine with me, and we'll go along together?"

"No, sir. I do not dine, lest it affront the spirits."

"Bozzy, Bozzy, clear your mind of humbug!"

"Miss Fan will have it so," I rejoined, sheepish but stubborn.

"Then so, I suppose, must it be. Well, well, I care not for the spirits. I'll have a cut off the joint, and make my way thither betimes."

As Dr. Johnson turned in at the fragrant doorway, I glanced just once over the hatch to where the spit turned at the fire, and then turned resolutely away to dine, as they say, with Duke Humphrey, which is to say, on air.

Yet when nearing midnight I presented myself at Miss Fanny Hall's door, there was no sign of Dr. Johnson. Firelight flickered, on sea-green panelling, on the sea-green damask sofa where sat Miss Fanny Hall, on the black shape of the wizard before the chimney-piece.

The wizard did not delay longer to make his preparations. First he presented a flask of his sovereign elixir.

"It will," he said, "so strengthen the vital fluid in your veins that you may laugh at any danger."

I set it to my lips. It tasted bitter. My lady choked over her glass. As the alchemist bent to aid her, I tipped my share quickly over the coals in the hod. Let my vital fluid take care of itself.

Next arrived the necessaries. There was fire on the hearth, earth in the Deathless One's scrip. Water arrived in a copper pitcher, air in the kitchen bellows, borne in upon a marble table by two serving-men in green baize aprons. One was a neat-built, clever-looking young-old fellow with a quizzical glance. I knew his face and nodded affably, getting a quiet smile and a sketched bow in return.

The other was a tall thick clown such as I had never before seen in Miss Fanny's service, louting low with many an obsequious scrape.

"This new fellow overplays his part," thought I, and looked again, and almost laughed, for he played a part indeed. Was I light-headed from hunger, or did I indeed see behind the green baize apron the majestic paunch of—Dr. Sam: Johnson! Was it come to this, that my common-sensical old friend should appear in his shirt-sleeves at midnight, as conjurer's acolyte and factotum to a wizard! His old friend Saint-Germain must be a warlock indeed!

The master ignored him. Mistress Fan signed the servants to be-gone. They went, but, I noted, no further than the curtained alcove, from which, as I knew to my cost, there was no egress—but that is another story.

"M. le Comte, we are ready."

The wizard turned the key in the lock.

"You have the necklace?"

The great pendant gems flashed in the firelight as their owner placed them in the copper bowl.

"There is great danger," said the conjurer solemnly, "more especially in the moment of fire. I beg that you will shield your eyes. You may use these masques."

We took the beak-nosed Venetian masques. The eye-holes were blocked. Secretly I resolved not to resort to mine. If Benvenuto Cellini could look upon a salamander, why not James Boswell?

The moment had come. The long deep strokes of midnight began to sound. On the last stroke the wizard opened his book, and the conjury began.

With elemental earth from his scrip, Saint-Germain the Deathless traced about himself on the marble floor three circles, pouring the dry dust in a thin stream between his long fingers. As he did so he muttered strange words:

"Spugliguel, Amaday, Abraym, Aguista, Yayn, Michaiel—Michaiel—Michaiel—"

This thrice-sacred word he traced on the circle with a strange cabbalistic device:

"Tilui, Caracasa Con, Amatiel, Commissoros . . ."

Suddenly there was a stench as of the Pit indeed: the wizard was making fumigations of sulphur. There was no light save the glow and reek of the fire, no sound save its secret voice. In the stillness the adept, tracing the holy pentacle, cried out aloud, invoking sacred names:

"By the mighty names of Adonay, El, Elohim, Elohe, Labaoth, Elion, Escerchie, Jah, Tetragrammaton, Saday—appear, assist!"

My head was reeling. I seemed to hear spiny wings rustle in red shadow above me, and spirit voices squeak in answer to their names. A black form against the fire in the grate, Saint-Germain bent over the copper bowl, lost in shadow before him.

"Aye, Seraye, aye, Seraye! El, Aty, Azia, Hin, Jen, Achaden, Vay! El, El, El, Hau, Hau, Hau, Va, Va, Va . . ."

I heard air sigh from the bellows; water lapped; then a shout: "Now! Beware the fire!"

He seized a blazing brand from the hearth and whirled it about, dashing it around his head, around the bowl, and around the protecting magick circle. Half-swooning, Miss Fan hid her eyes; but mine, open, beheld the great red blaze that sheeted up, so that the distorted face in the ring of fire gleamed like a demon's in Hell. Then his hand shot up above the dwindling blaze to wave in triumph—the necklace we conjured for. Thus he stood till the red fire had died to the floor. Then he stepped forward and laid a much augmented necklace in milady's hand.

"I have obeyed your command," he said. "I am exhausted in blood and spirit. Thank me, and let me go."

"A moment," said Dr. Sam: Johnson, stepping from the alcove.

Saint-Germain whirled.

"You have betrayed me!" he cried angrily. "You have put spies on me!"

"I, set spies?" protested Miss Fan. "Are not these your people?"

"My people? I have no people. I desired your butler to send up air and water, and supposed the bearers to be your footmen."

"I am no footman," said Dr. Johnson. "I am Sam: Johnson, at your service, ma'am, and I have a mind to conjure on my own account."

"Stand back, fellow!" cried the wizard angrily. "Take care, the spirits may do you an injury; and if they do not, I will!"

He was a menacing figure, rearing black and tall in the firelight. But Dr. Sam: Johnson stood as tall, and bulkier. With one powerful thrust he shouldered the threatening magus aside.

"By your leave, sir, my conjury is soon done. Ducdame! Ducdame! Ducdame! Honorificabilitudinitatibus!"

At each of these oddly-chosen incantations he took a handful of magick earth from the scrip on the table. The first two he scattered in a ring. The third, from the left hand, he broadcast widdershins. The fourth he flung on the fire, where it exploded in a sheet of crimson flame. Above the inferno, Dr. Johnson's great left hand brandished—a diamond necklace.

The Deathless One was at the door; but the key was no longer in the lock. By the door the second attendant stood smiling to himself. Saint-Germain shrugged, and turned back. The little man in the green baize apron stepped forward and took the augmented necklace from Mistress Fanny's hand.

"By your leave, Madame," he said. "I have some skill as a lapidary."

I stared at the speaker as he fixed a jeweller's glass in his eye. So my friend had fetched along a lapidary. I had been foolish in taking that quietly commanding face for a servant's; but if not above a green baize apron, where had I seen that quizzical glance before?

As he studied the augmented necklace, motionless, Dr. Sam: Johnson officiously used his green apron to dust the necklace he had conjured up. Then it in its turn came under the scrutiny of the jeweller's glass. Something held us all silent. At last:

"This necklace," said the lapidary, extending the augmented collar, "is paste; paste made by a master, but paste. These—" tendering the smaller necklace—"are right diamonds—"

"Being," put in Johnson, "in fact your own Golconda stones, which this scoundrel would have carried off in his scripful of red fire, had not I conjured it forth again."

"What!" ejaculated Miss Fanny, unready to believe, "the famous Comte de Saint-Germain, the Deathless One, a charlatan and a thief?"

"He is not the Comte de Saint-Germain. He is Andrew Hopper, formerly diamond-cutter to Brouwere of Amsterdam."

"This fellow is mad," said the tall alchemist loftily.

"Mrs. Cornelys admits the imposture—"

"I thought she was mighty pat with her part, like one that had conned it!" cried I.

"When taxed with it, she just laughs, and says there is no harm in it. Andrew Hopper was ever a quiz, she says, and his jest will pay out Mistress Hall for her pride, which ill becomes a h—hem, which ill becomes her."

"Says she so?" muttered Mistress Fan, and looked like a thunder cloud.

"I came incognito," said the wizard. "Shall I blab my name to the first footman that asks it? I am the Comte de Saint-Germain."

"You are Andrew Hopper," retorted Dr. Johnson. "You fled from Amsterdam having stolen from Brouwere's coffers this necklace—" he dangled it contemptuously—"which is the paste pattern Brouwere made for the Empress; and with it you came to England, of purpose to cozen Mistress Hall by the hocus-pocus we have seen."

"All lies. I am the Comte de Saint-Germain."

"I cry a thousand pardons," said the little lapidary softly. "I am desolated to say it; but, sir, you lie. You are not the Comte de Saint-Germain."

"How are you so sure, my little man?" demanded the wizard.

"Because I am the Comte de Saint-Germain."

"You?" cried Mistress Fan. "You, Saint-Germain the Deathless?"

"Yes, I, madame, at your service. When I saw in the English newspapers that the Comte de Saint-Germain was in London, when I knew I was at Amsterdam; and moreover that diamonds were to be conjured in my name; I hastened across the Channel. Putting up incognito at the Cross Keys, I walked straight into the arms of my old friend here, who informed me of what had already passed. Together we observed the false Comte, and I recognized Andrew Hopper, who had mystified Amsterdam when he absconded with so many false stones, and one right diamond only—"

"To begin the plot if need be," struck in Dr. Johnson, "with a right diamond, that should reassure the lady, and get the necklace into his hands."

"When we had heard Mrs. Cornelys, I would have exposed the charlatan at once; but my old friend here was for catching him red-handed at his jugglery."

"How did you appear so pat, then?" inquired milady.

"Money opened the way at your kitchen door, where indeed our only difficulty lay in perswading milady's woman to conduct us, not to milady's bedchamber, but to the scene of the conjury—and such conjury! Really, monsieur, such puerilities will do my reputation scant credit! Whence had you this hodge-podge, fellow?" From the table he took the wizard's book. "Pietro d'Albano! Give me leave to say, my friend, that you took great risks in summoning Michaiel on a Tuesday, and with fumigations of sulphur besides! This it is to copy at random from a book you do not understand! Not that Dr. Johnson's cantrips were any better. What is this 'Ducdame?'"

"As the wise Shakespeare will have it—an invocation to call fools into a circle," replied Dr. Johnson with a grin. "Let my cantrips be what they will, you'll admit I conjured forth the right gems."

"By what magic did you so?" I asked him.

"By observing. Let a man use his eyes, he may penetrate mysteries not revealed in the *Golden Chain of Homer,* the Great nor the Little Albert, nor the mysterious volume of Picatrix."

"What did you observe?"

"That the false conjurer's hands went never to his pockets, many times to his scrip, the only thing upon the table in which, being his, he might carry away a prize. It was thence, while we were dazzled by his *feu d'artifice,* that he must have produced the false necklace, and there he must have hidden the true one. I groped for it, drew it on the third cast forth, and there it is."

"Is the comedy ended?" demanded the unabashed impostor. "If so, I will bid you good night."

"Shall I fetch the constables?" I cried.

"The constables? What have they to do here? I have amused the company by my art, and the performance is at an end. It was nothing but an evening's pastime."

"Nothing!" I cried hotly. "Is theft nothing!"

"Theft? What have I stolen?" demanded the charlatan coolly. "Ah, yes, theft. It is true that in the course of these proceedings the harlot here has cozened me out of a valuable diamond, for which she could be branded on the hand—"

"Branded!" shrieked Miss Fanny Hall. "Unlock the door!"

"—but I give it her, and the paste necklace to boot, and so I take my leave—" (as Dr. Johnson flung wide the door) "—and may the Devil fly away with the lot of you!"

"*Ma foi,*" said the true Count in his soft, sonorous voice, "what a species of a pork, to pass for the Comte de Saint-Germain!"

"Monsieur le Comte," breathed Miss Fanny Hall, seating him graciously, green baize apron and all, by her side on the sea-green damask sofa, "is it true that you will live forever?"

"That, madame," he replied with his quiet smile, "remains to be seen."

"And pray, Count," she wheedled, fingering the stones of her restored necklace, "is it true as they say—"

Observing the thunder clouds gathering on my brow, to see myself once more slighted, Dr. Johnson with a grim jerk of his head recalled me to myself and haled me forth of the room; but the mellifluous coaxing voice floated after us:

"Is it true, Count, that you can augment the size of diamonds?"

[The historical Saint-Germain once presented the French King with a diamond which, he said, he had magically re-made. He is not known to have met Johnson. Certain esoteric sects still think he is immortal, because they believe they have seen him recently.]

THE MISSING SHAKESPEARE MANUSCRIPT

(*Stratford-on-Avon, 1769*)

'Twas Dr. Sam: Johnson, in the end, who restored the missing Shakespeare manuscript at the Stratford Jubilee in the year 1769; though in the beginning he would not so much as look at it. In that rainy September, he preferred to hug the fire at the Red Lion Inn.

There he stood, bulky and immovable, holding forth his large, well-shaped hands to the glow of the coals and turning a deaf ear to my perswasions. But if he was stubborn, I was pertinacious.

"Do, Dr. Johnson," I urged, "give me your company to Mr. Ararat's though you come but to scoff."

"I shall not remain to pray, I promise you," rejoined the great Cham of literature intransigeantly.

"So much is unnecessary," I replied, "but indeed I have promised we would meet there with Dr. Percy and his young friend Malone, the Irish lawyer."

"This is very proper for Thomas Percy and his scavenging friends," remarked Dr. Johnson, lifting his coat-tails before the blaze, "for they are very methodists in the antiquarian *enthusiasm*. But truly this is ill for a scholar, to run with the vulgar after a parcel of old waste paper."

"Sir, sir," I protested, "the antiquarian zeal of Mr. Ararat has preserved to us a previously unknown tragedy of Shakespeare, 'Caractacus; or, the British Hero'."

"Which little Davy Garrick is to represent in the great amphitheatre tomorrow night. Let him do so. Let us see him do so. Let us not meddle with the musty reliques of the writing desk."

"Musty!" I cried. "Let me tell you this is no musty old dog's-eared folio that has lost its wrappings for pyes or worse, like the ballad-writings Percy cherishes, but a manuscript as fair and unblemished, so Dr. Warton assures me, as the day it came from the bard's own hand. By singular good luck Mr. Ararat is of antiquarian mind, and the manuscript was preserved from a noisome fate in the out-house."

"That it was preserved for Garrick to play and Dodsley to publish, this is luck indeed; but now that the playhouse copies are taken off, it may end in the out-house for all of me," replied my learned friend. "No, sir; let a good play be well printed and well played; but to idolize mere paper and ink is rank superstition and idolatry."

"Why, sir, you need not adore it, nor look at it if you will not; but pray let us not disappoint Dr. Percy and his young friend."

Dr. Johnson's good nature was not proof against this appeal to friendship; he consented to walk along with me to Mr. Ararat's.

I made haste to don my hat and be off before anything could supervene. As we set off on foot from the yard of the Red Lion, my revered friend peered at me with puckered eyes.

"Pray, Mr. Boswell," he enquired in tones of forced forbearance, "what is the writing inserted in your hat?"

I doffed the article in question and gazed admiringly at the neatly inscribed legend which adorned it.

"CORSICA BOSWELL," read off my learned friend in tones of disgust. "Corsica Boswell! Pray, what commodity are you touting, Mr. Boswell, that you advertize the world of your name in this manner?"

"A very precious commodity," I retorted with spirit, "liberty for down-trodden Corsica. Do but attend the great masquerade tonight, you shall see how I speak for Corsica."

"Well, sir, you may speak for whom you will, and advertize Stratford of your name as you please. For me, let me remain *incognito*. I should be loath to parade about Stratford as DICTIONARY JOHNSON."

"Say rather," I replied, "as SHAKESPEARE JOHNSON, for your late edition of the Bard must endear you to the town of his birth."

"I come to Stratford," remarked Dr. Johnson with finality, "to observe men and manners, and not to tout for my wares."

"Be it so," I replied, "here is material most proper for your observation."

As I spoke, we were crossing the public square, which teemed with bewildered Stratfordians and jostling strangers. The center of a milling crowd, a trumpeter was splitting the air with his blasts and loudly proclaiming:

"Ladies and gentlemen! The famous Sampson is just going to begin—just going to mount four horses at once with his feet upon two saddles—also the most wonderful surprizing feats of horsemanship by the most *notorious* Mrs. Sampson."

A stringy man and an Amazon of a woman seconded his efforts by giving away inky bills casting further light on their own notorious feats. As we strolled on, we met a man elbowing his way through the press beating a drum and shouting incessantly:

"The notified Porcupine Man, and all sorts of outlandish birds and other beasts to be seen without loss of time on the great meadow near the amphitheatre at so small a price as one shilling a piece. Alive, alive, alive, ho."

Behind him came a man leading a large bin, and a jostling crowd following. Dr. Johnson smiled.

"This foolish fellow will scarce make his fortune at the Jubilee," he remarked. "Who will pay a shilling to see strange animals in a house, when a man may see them for nothing going along the streets, alive, alive, ho?"

As we walked along, Dr. Johnson marvelled much at the elegant art of the decorations displayed about the town. The town hall was adorned with five transparencies on silk—in the center Shakespeare, flanked by Lear and Caliban, Falstaff and Pistol. The humble cottage where Shakespeare was born, gave me those feelings which men of enthusiasm have on seeing remarkable places; and I had a solemn and serene satisfaction in contemplating the church in which his body lies.

Dr. Johnson, however, took a more lively interest in the untutored artistry of the townsfolk of Stratford, who had everywhere adorned their houses, according to their understanding and fantasy, in honour of their Bard. We read many a rude legend displayed to the glorification of Shakespeare and Warwickshire. We beheld many a crude portrait intended for the great playwright, and only a few less libels on the lineaments of David Garrick, as we strolled down to Mr. Ararat's.

"This is Garrick's misfortune, that as steward of the Jubilee, he is man of the hour," remarked Dr. Johnson, "for the admiration of Warwickshire has done him no less wrong than the lampoons of London."

"In Shakespeare he has a notable fellow-sufferer," I replied.

Johnson "You say true, Bozzy. Alack, Bozzy, do my eyes inform me true as to the nature of the small building, set apart, which someone has seen fit to adorn with the honoured features of the Bard?"

Boswell "Your eyes inform you truly. We are approaching the stationer's shop of Mr. Ararat, whose zeal for Shakespeare extends even to adorning the exterior of his out-house with the counterfeit presentment of the Bard."

Johnson "Better his face without than his works within."

Boswell "Sir, the antiquarian zeal of Mr. Ararat, 'tis said, extends even so far, for he provides for the convenience of his household a pile of old accounts of wonderful and hoary antiquity. The Stratfordians are long dead and gone who bought the paper for which the reckoning still awaits a last usefulness."

Johnson "Let Mr. Ararat keep Thomas Percy out of here. Last year he published the Earl of Northumberland's reckonings for bread and cheese from the year 1512; next year, unless he's watched, I'll be bound, he'll rush to the press with a parcel of stationer's accounts he's *borrowed* from Ararat's out-house."

Boswell "Sir, you wrong Thomas Percy. He's a notable antiquarian and his works are much sought after."

Johnson "He's a snapper-up of unconsidered trifles, and that young Irishman who's followed him hither is no better. Sir, be it a Shakespeare manuscript or a publican's reckoning, just so it be old, I'd watch it narrowly while Percy is about."

Speaking thus, we turned the corner, when the full complexity of Mr. Ararat's decorative scheme struck us at once. Limned by an unskillful hand, the characters of Shakespeare's plays crowded the ancient facade, dominated under the gabled roof by the lineaments of the Bard, for which the portrait on the necessary-house was clearly a preliminary study. Hamlet leaned a melancholy elbow on the steep gable of the window, Macbeth and Macduff fought with claymores over the front door, a giant warrior guarded the corner post, all endued with a weird kind of life in the gray glare of the sky, for a storm was threatening.

"Ha," said Dr. Johnson, "who is this painted chieftain? Can it be Cymbeline?"

"No, sir, this is Caractacus, hero of the new play just recovered."

Johnson "Why has he painted himself like an Onondaga?"

Boswell "Sir, he is an ancient Briton. He has painted himself with woad."

Johnson "Will little Davy Garrick paint himself blue?"

Boswell "I cannot say, sir, though 'tis known he means to present the character in ancient British dress."

Johnson "This is more of your *antiquarianism*. Let Davy Garrick but present a *man*, he may despise the fribbles of the tiring-room."

As we thus stood chatting before the stationer's shop, a strange creature insinuated himself before us. From his shoulder depended a tray full of oddments.

"Tooth pick cases, needle cases, punch ladles, tobacco stoppers, inkstands, nutmeg graters, and all sorts of boxes, made out of the famous mulberry tree," he chanted.

"Pray, sir, shall we venture?"

"Nay, Bozzy, the words of the bard are the true metal, his mulberry tree is but dross. You seem determined to make a papistical idolator of me."

"Yet perhaps this box—" I indicated a wooden affair large enough for a writing desk—"this box is sufficiently useful in itself—"

With a resentful scowl the man snatched it rudely from my hand. "'Tis not for sale," he mumbled, and ran down the street with his boxes hopping.

"Are all the people mad?" quoted Dr. Johnson from the "Comedy of Errours"; and the shop bell tinkled to herald our entrance into the stationer's shop of Mr. Ararat.

Behind the counter in the dim little shop stood a solid-built man in a green baize apron. He had a sanguine face and thin, gingery hair. This was Mr. Ararat, stationer of Stratford, Shakespearean enthusiast, and owner of the precious manuscript of "Caractacus;

or, the British Hero." He spelled out the sign on my hat and gave me a low bow.

"Welcome, Mr. Boswell, to you and your friend."

We greeted Mr. Ararat with suitable distinction. Being made known to Dr. Johnson, he greeted him with surprised effusion.

"This is indeed an unlooked-for honour, Dr. Johnson," cried Mr. Ararat.

"Percy is late," I observed to Dr. Johnson.

"Dr. Percy was here, and has but stepped out for a moment," Mr. Ararat informed us.

We whiled away the time of waiting by examining the honest stationer's stock, and Dr. Johnson purchased some of his laid paper, much to my surprise to good advantage. As the parcel was wrapping Thomas Percy put his long nose in at the door, and followed it by his neat person attired in clerical black. He laid his parcel on the counter and took Dr. Johnson by both his hands.

"We must count ourselves fortunate," he cried, "to have attracted Dr. Johnson hither. I had feared we could never lure you from Brighthelmstone, where the witty and fair conspired to keep you."

"Why, sir, the witty and fair, if by those terms you mean to describe Mrs. Thrale, took a whim that the sea air gave her a megrim, and back she must post to Streatham; and I took a whim not to wait upon her whims, so off I came for Stratford."

"We are the gainers," cried Percy.

Dr. Johnson's eye fell on the counter, where lay his package of paper and the exactly similar parcel Percy had laid down. He picked up the latter.

"Honest Mr. Ararat does well by us Londoners," he remarked, "to sell us fine paper so cheap."

"Yes, sir," replied Percy, possessing himself of his parcel with more haste than was strictly mannerly, "you see I know how to prize new folios as well as old, ha ha."

He gripped his parcel, and during the whole of our exciting transactions in the house of Mr. Ararat it never left his hands again.

At that moment the shop-bell tinkled to admit a stranger. I saw a fresh-faced Irishman with large spiritual eyes the colour of brook water, a straight nose long at the tip, and a delicate smiling mouth.

He was shabbily dressed in threadbare black. The new-comer nodded to Percy, and made a low bow to my venerable friend.

"Your servant, Dr. Johnson," he exclaimed in a soft mellifluous voice. "Permit me to recall myself—Edmond Malone, at your service I had the honour to be made known to you some years since by my countryman Edmund Southwell."

"I remember it well," replied Dr. Johnson cordially, "'Twas at the Grecian, in the Strand. I had a kindness for Southwell."

"He will be happy to hear it," replied Malone.

'Twas thus that I, James Boswell, the Scottish advocate, not quite twenty-nine, met Edmond Malone, the Irish lawyer, then in the twenty-eighth year of his age, who was destined to become—but I digress.

Our party being complete, we repaired into the inner room and were accommodated with comfortable chairs. Seated by the chimney-piece was a boy of about sixteen, a replica of old Mr. Ararat, with a rough red mop of hair and peaked red eyebrows. He looked at us without any expression on his round face.

"'Tis Anthony," said his father with pride, "Anthony's a good boy."

"What do you read so diligently, my lad?" enquired Dr. Johnson kindly, peering at the book the boy held. "Johnson's *Shakespeare!* I am honoured!"

"Nay, sir, 'tis we who are honoured," said Malone fervently. "To inspect the Shakespeare manuscript in the company of him who knows the most in England of the literature of our country and the plays of the Bard, to read the literature of yesterday in the presence of Dictionary Johnson, who knows the age and lineage of every English word from the oldest to the word minted but yesterday, this is to savour the fine flower of scholarship."

The red-haired boy turned his eyes toward Dr. Johnson.

"Pray, sir," replied Dr. Johnson, "don't cant. In restoring a lost play this worthy boy has deserved as well as I of his fellow-Englishmen."

"Anthony's a good boy," said his father with pride, "he knows the plays of Shakespeare by heart, 'Caractacus' included."

I looked at Anthony, and doubted it.

"Shall you make him a stationer, like his fathers before him?" enquired Dr. Percy politely.

"No, sir," replied Ararat, "he's prenticed to old Mr. Quiney the scrivener over the way. Here, Anthony, fetch my strong-box, we'll show the gentleman what they came to see."

Anthony nodded, and went quickly out of the room.

"This is a great good fortune," said Dr. Percy eagerly, "to see the very writing of Shakespeare himself. We are your debtors that it has been preserved."

"'Tis nothing," but old Ararat began to swell like a turkey-cock. He launched into the story: "The first Anthony Ararat was a stationer in Stratford, like me, and Will Shakespeare was his neighbour. Anthony saved his life in the Avon, and in recompense he had of Will the manuscript of this very play, 'Caractacus; or, the British Hero', to be his and his children's forever. Old Anthony knew how to value it, for he folded it in silk, and laid with it a writing of how he came by it, and laid it away with his accounts and private papers."

"Then how came it to be lost?" enquired Dr. Percy.

"'Twas my grandmother, sir, who took the besom to all the old papers together, and bundled one with another into the shed, and there they lay over the years with the lumber and the stationer's trash. I played in there when I was a boy, and so did Anthony after me. I remember, there was paper in there my father said his grandfather had made when he was prenticed in the paper-mills. But I never turned over the old accountings, nor paid them any heed. But to make a long story short, gentlemen, come Jubilee time I thought to turn an honest penny letting lodgings, so I bade Anthony turn out the lumber in the shed and make a place where the horses could stand. Anthony turned out a quantity of waste paper and lumber, and my mother's marriage lines that went missing in the '28, and the manuscript of 'Caractacus', wrapped in silk as the first Anthony had laid it by. He had the wit to bring it to me, and I took it over to old Mr. Quiney the engrosser, and between us we soon made out what we had. Warton of Trinity rode over from

Oxford, and Mr. Garrick came down from London and begged to play it . . ."

The words died in his throat. I followed his gaze toward the inner door. There stood young Anthony, pale as death. Tears were streaming down his wet face. Angrily he dashed the drops from his shoulder. In his hand he held a brass-bound coffer, about the size of the mulberry-wood box the pedlar had snatched from us. Wordlessly, though his throat constricted, he held out the strong-box toward his father. It was empty. We saw the red silk lining, and the contorted metal where the lock had been forced.

The manuscript of "Caractacus" had vanished quite away.

Old Ararat was beside himself. Thomas Percy was racked between indignation and pure grief. Only Dr. Johnson maintained a philosophical calm.

"Pray, Mr. Ararat, compose yourself. Remember the playhouse copies are safely taken off. You have lost no more than a parcel of waste paper."

"But, sir," cried Malone, "the very hand of the Bard!"

"And a very crabbed hand too," rejoined Johnson, "old Quiney over the way will engross you a better for a crown."

"But, pray, Dr. Johnson," I enquired, "is not its value enormous?"

"Its value is nil. 'Tis so well-known, and so unique, that the thief can never sell it; he can only feed his fancy, that it is now his. Let him gloat. 'Caractacus' is ours. Tomorrow we shall see Garrick play the British hero; the day after tomorrow it will be given to the world in an elegant edition. The thief has gained, Mr. Ararat has lost, nothing but old paper."

But Percy and the Ararats thought otherwise. We deployed like an army through the domain of the good stationer, and left no corner unsearched. We had up the red satin lining of the coffer; we turned over the stationer's stock-in-trade; we searched the house from top to bottom; all to no purpose. In the end we went away without finding anything, leaving young Anthony stupefied by the chimney-piece and old Ararat red with rage and searching, blaming the whole thing on the Jubilee.

We were a dreary party as we walked back to the Red Lion in the rain. Percy and Malone stalked on in heart-broken silence. Having given his parcel into Percy's keeping, Dr. Johnson swayed along muttering to himself and touching the palings as we passed. Alone retaining my wonted spirits, I broached in vain half a dozen cheerful topicks, and at last fell silent like the rest.

Arrived in the court-yard of the Red Lion, Dr. Johnson took his parcel from Percy's hand and vanished without a word. I lingered long enough to take a dram for the prevention of the ague. Percy and Malone were sorry company, quaffing in silence by my side, and soon by mutual consent we parted to shift our wet raiment.

In the chamber I shared with Dr. Johnson (dubbed, according to the fancy of Mr. Peyton the landlord, after one of Shakespeare's plays, "Much Ado about Nothing") I found my venerable friend, shifted to dry clothing, muffled in a counterpane and staring at the fire.

I ventured to enquire where in his opinion the sacred document had got to.

"Why, Bozzy," replied he, "some Shakespeare-maniac has got it, you may depend upon it, or as it might be, some old-paper maniac. Some scavenging antiquarian has laid hold of it and gloats over it in secret."

"I cry your pardon," said Dr. Percy, suddenly appearing at our door. He was white and uneasy still. In his hand he carried a parcel. "Pray, Dr. Johnson, do you not have my parcel that I brought from Mr. Ararat's?"

"I, Dr. Percy? I have my own parcel." Dr. Johnson indicated it where it lay still wrapped on the table.

Percy seized it, and scrutinized the wrappings narrowly.

"You are deceived, Dr. Johnson. This parcel is mine. Here is yours, which I retained in errour for my own. I fear I have disarranged it in opening. Pray forgive me. I see you have opened mine more neatly."

" 'Tis as I had it of you," replied Dr. Johnson.

"You have not opened it!" cried Percy. "Well, Dr. Johnson, now we each have our own again, and no harm's done, eh? We lovers of good paper have done a shrewd day's bargaining, have we not, ha ha ha!"

"I will wager mine was the better bargain," said Dr. Johnson good-humouredly. "Come, open up, let us see."

"No, no, Dr. Johnson, I must be off," and Percy whipped through the door before either of us could say a word.

"Now," remarked Dr. Johnson, "'tis seen that Peyton was well advised to name our chamber 'Much Ado about Nothing'."

The rain continued in a dreary stream, so that boards had to be laid over the kennel to transport the ladies dry-shod into the amphitheatre; but for all that, the great masquerade that night was surely the finest entertainment of the kind ever witnessed in Britain. I was sorry that Dr. Johnson elected to miss it. There were many rich, elegant, and curious dresses, many beautiful women, and some characters well supported. Three ladies personated Macbeth's three witches with devastating effect, while a person dressed as the devil gave inexpressible offence.

I own, however, that 'twas my own attire that excited the most remark. Appearing in the character of an armed Corsican chief, I wore a short, dark-coloured coat of coarse cloth, scarlet waistcoat and breeches, and black spatterdashes, and a cap of black cloth, bearing on its front, embroidered in gold letters, VIVA LA LIBERTA, and on its side a blue feather and cockade. I also wore a cartridge-pouch, into which was stuck a stiletto, and on my left side a pistol. A musket was slung across my shoulder, and my black hair, unpowdered, hung plaited down my neck, ending in a knot of blue ribbands. In my right hand I carried a long vine staff, with a bird curiously carved at the long curving upper end, emblematical of the sweet bard of Avon. In this character of a Corsican chief I delivered a poetical address on the united subjects of Corsica and the Stratford Jubilee.

I cannot forbear to rehearse the affecting peroration:

"But let me plead for LIBERTY distrest,
And warm for her each sympathetick Breast:
Amongst the splendid Honours which you bear,
To save a Sister Island! be your Care:
With generous Ardour make US also FREE;
And give to CORSICA, a NOBLE JUBILEE."

As I came to an applauded close, I heard a resonant voice at my elbow.

"Pray, Bozzy," demanded Dr. Johnson, peering at me with disfavour, "what is the device on your coat? The head of a blackamoor upon a charger, garnished with watercress?"

"That, sir," I replied stiffly, "is the crest of Corsica, a Moor's head surrounded by branches of laurel. But what brings you from your bed, whither you were bound when I left you?"

"Sir," replied Dr. Johnson, "somebody in Stratford is in possession of the missing manuscript of Mr. Ararat. Here I have them all gathered under one roof, and all out of character, or into another character, which is just as revealing. I am here to observe. Let us retire into this corner and watch how they go on. To him who will see with his eyes, all secrets are open."

"Tooth pick cases, needle cases, punch ladles, tobacco stoppers, inkstands, nutmeg graters, and all sorts of boxes, made out of the famous mulberry tree," chanted a musical voice behind us. We turned to behold the very figure of the man with the tray. His brilliant eyes twinkled behind his mask.

"Goods from the mulberry tree," he chanted, "made out of old chairs and stools and stained according, tooth pick cases, needle cases, punch ladles—"

A blast from a trumpet cut him off. Beside him stood a second mask, garbed "like Rumour painted full of tongues," impersonating Fame with trumpet and scroll.

"Pray, sir," said Dr. Johnson, entering into the spirit of the occasion, "let us glimpse your scroll, whether our names be not inscribed thereon."

The mask withheld the scroll, and spoke in a husky voice:

"Nay, sir, my scroll is blank."

"Why, sir, then you are the prince of cynics. What, not one name? Not *Corsica* Boswell? Not Garrick? Not Shakespeare? Sir, were I to betray this to the Corporation, you should stand in the pillory."

"Therefore I shall not reveal myself—even to Dr. Johnson—" replied the mask in his husky voice. He would have slipped away, when one of those spasmodic movements which cause my venerable friend so much distress hurled to the ground both trumpet and scroll. In a contest of courtesy, Fame retrieved the trumpet and my venerable friend the scroll.

"You say true," remarked the last-named sadly, re-rolling the scroll, "on the roster of Fame, my name is not inscribed."

He restored the scroll with a bow, and Fame made off with the mulberry-wood vendor.

"I interest myself much in the strange personages of this assemblage," remarked my philosophical friend. "Alack, there's a greater guy than you, *Corsica* Boswell, for he's come out without his breeches."

I recognized with surprize the fiery mop and blank face of young Ararat, whom I had last seen that morning weeping for the lost manuscript. He was robed in white linen, and carried scrip and claymore. He wore no mask, but his face was daubed with blue.

"'Tis Anthony,' said I, "he personates Caractacus, the British hero. Sure he trusts in vain if he thinks to conceal his identity behind a little blue paint."

"To the man with eyes, the heaviest mask is no concealment," replied Dr. Johnson; "sure you smoaked our friends with the scroll and the mulberry wood in spite of their valences."

"Not I, trust me. Fame's husky voice was no less strange to me than the wizened figure of the pedlar."

"The husky voice, the bent figure, were assumed for disguise," replied Dr. Johnson, "but Percy's long nose was plain for all to see, and Malone's mellifluous tones were no less apparent. They thought to quiz me; but I shall quiz them tomorrow."

I was watching young Ararat, with his father the center of a sycophantic group of masks who made *lions* of them. Young Anthony was as impassive as ever, but his face was as red as his father's. Lady Macbeth plucked at his elbow; the three Graces fawned upon him; in the press about him I saw the trumpet of Fame and the tray of the mulberry pedlar.

"A springald Caractacus," remarked Dr. Johnson, following my gaze, "how long, think you, could he live in equal combat if his life depended on that dull-edged claymore?"

"Yet see," I commented severely, "how the ladies flatter him, whose only claim on their kindness amounts to this, that through no merit of his own he found a dusty bundle of papers in his father's shed."

"While those who can compose, ay and declaim, verses upon *liberty*," supplied Dr. Johnson slyly, "stand neglected save by a musty old scholar."

"Nay, sir," I protested; but Dr. Johnson cut me off:

"Why, sir, we are all impostors here. Fame with an empty scroll, mulberry wood cut from old chairs and stools! Sir, I have canvassed the abilities of the company, and I find that but one sailor out of six can dance a horn-pipe, and but one more box his compass. Not one conjuror can inform me whether he could tell my fortune better by chiromancy or catoptromancy. None of four farmers knows how a score of runts sells now; and the harlequin is as stiff as a poker. So your Caractacus is an impostor among impostors, and we must not ask too much of him."

I looked at the press around the finder and the owner of the missing manuscript, buzzing like bees with talk and laughter. There was a sudden silence, broken by a bellow from old Ararat. The buzzing began again on a higher note, and the whole swarm bore down on our corner, old Ararat in the lead. He brandished in his hand an open paper.

Wordlessly he extended the paper to my friend. Peering over his shoulder, I read with him:

"Sir,

The manuscript of Caractacus is safe, and I have a mind to profit from it in spite of your teeth. Lay £100 in the font at the church, and you shall hear further.

Look to it; for if the value of the manuscript is nil, and profits me nothing, as God is my judge I will destroy it. I do not steal in sport.

I am,

Sir,

Your obliged humble servant,

Ignotus"

"The scoundrel!" cried old Ararat. "Where am I to find £100?"

"This is more of your antiquarianism," I remarked, "like a knight of old, the miscreant holds his captive to *ransom*."

Dr. Johnson turned the letter in his hands, and held it against the lights of the great chandelier. 'Twas writ in a fair hand on ordinary laid paper, and sealed with yellow wax; but instead of using a seal, the unknown writer had set his thumb in the soft wax.

"Why," says he, "the thief has signed himself with *hand* and *seal* indeed. Now were there but some way to match this seal to the thumb that made it, we should lay the robber by the heels and have back the manuscript that Shakespeare wrote."

"Alack, sir," I replied, "there is no way."

"Nevertheless, let us try," said Dr. Johnson sturdily. "Pray, Mr. Malone, set your thumb in this seal."

"I?" said the mulberry-wood pedlar, drawing back.

"I will," said I, and set my thumb in the waxen matrix. It fitted perfectly. The eyes of the maskers turned to me, and I felt my ears burning. Dr. Johnson held out the seal to old Ararat, who with a stormy mutter of impatience tried to crowd his huge thumb into the impression. 'Twas far too broad.

Dr. Johnson tried in turn the thumb of each masker. The ladies' thumbs were too slender, Malone's too long; but there were many in the group that fitted. Dr. Johnson shook his head.

"This is the fallacy of the undistributed middle term" said he. "Some other means must be found than gross measurement, to fit a thumb to the print it makes. Pray, how came you by this letter?"

"'Twas tossed at my feet by someone in the press," replied old Ararat. "Come, Dr. Johnson, advise me, how am I to come by £100 to buy back my lost manuscript?"

"A subscription!" cried Fame. "The price is moderate for so precious a prize. I myself will undertake to raise the sum for you."

So it was concerted. Dr. Johnson enjoined secrecy upon the maskers, and Fame with his visor off, revealed as Dr. Percy indeed, bustled off to open the subscription books.

We lay late the next day in the "Much Ado about Nothing" chamber. Dr. Johnson was given over to indolence, and declined to say what he had learned at the masquerade, or whether he thought that the mysterious communication held out any hope that the missing manuscript might be recovered.

The rain continuing, the pageant was dispensed with. We whiled away the hours comfortably at the Red Lion, while Percy and Malone spent a damp day with their subscription books. Representing the collection merely as "for the Ararats," they found the sum of £100 not easy to be amassed. Toward evening, however, they returned to the Red Lion with £87 in silver and copper, and Garrick's promise to make up the sum when the play's takings should be counted.

Dr. Johnson spurned at the idea of buying back mere paper and faded ink. In his roaring voice he *tossed* and *gored* Dr. Percy for his magpie love of old documents, adverting especially to Percy's recent publication of "The Household Book of the Earls of Northumberland."

"Pray, sir," he demanded with scorn, "of what conceivable utility to mankind can the 'Household Book' be supposed to be? The world now knows that a dead-and-gone Percy had beef to the value of twelve pence on a Michaelmas in 1512. Trust me, 'twill set no beef on the table of any living Percy."

The young Irish lawyer came to the unfortunate clergyman's defense, and fared no better. Johnson was in high good spirits as we dined off a veal pye and a piece of good beef (which the living Percy relished well).

We then repaired to the amphitheatre, where Percy had concerted to meet the Ararats with Caractacus's ransom.

Old Ararat would have none of Dr. Johnson's advice, to ignore Ignotus's letter. He was hot to conclude the business, and would hear of no other plan, than to deposit the £100 in the font as soon as the play should be over and the takings counted.

"Then, sir," said Dr. Johnson in disgust, "at least let us entrap Ignotus, and make him Gnotus. Mr. Boswell and I will watch by the font and take him as he comes for his ill-gotten gains."

"We must stand watch and watch," cried Percy. "Malone and I will relieve you."

"Nay, let me," cried old Ararat.

"So be it," assented Dr. Johnson; and we repaired to our respective boxes to see the play.

We shared a box with Percy and Malone. Dr. Johnson grunted to himself when David Garrick made his first entrance on the battlements, wearing white linen kilts and bedaubed with blue paint. In spite of this antiquarianism, I found myself moved deeply by the noble eloquence, the aweful elevation of soul, with which Garrick spoke the words of this play so strangely preserved for our generation. I was most affected by the solemn soliloquy which concluded the first act:

"O sovereign death,
Thou hast for thy domain this world immense:
Churchyards and charnel-houses are thy haunts,
And hospitals thy sumptuous palaces;
And when thou would'st be merry, thou dost chuse
The gaudy chamber of a dying King.
O! Then thou dost ope wide thy boney jaw
And with rude laughter and fantastick tricks,
Thou clapp'st thy rattling fingers to thy sides:
And when this solemn mockery is o'er,
With icy hand thou tak'st him by the feet,
And upward so, till thou dost reach the heart,
And wrap him in the cloak of lasting night."

As the act ended, from the stage box the Ararats, father and son, rose to share the plaudits of the huzzaing crowd.

"Davy Garrick," remarked Dr. Johnson in my ear, "has surpassed himself; and King is inimitable as the Fool."

The second act opened with another scene of King's.

"Alack," cries the lovelorn Concairn,
"Alack, I will write verses of my love,
They shall be hung on every tree . . ."

King turned a cart-wheel, ending with a resounding smack on the rump.

"Say rather," he cried, "they shall be used in every jakes, for by'r lakin, such fardels does thy prentice hand compose, they are as caviare to the mob. I can but compliment thee thus, they do go to the *bottom* of the matter."

The pit roared.

"Ha, what?" exclaimed Dr. Johnson. "Bozzy, Bozzy, where's my hat?"

"Your hat, sir? Why, the play is not half over."

Dr. Johnson fumbled around in the dark.

"No matter. Do you stay and see it through. Where's this hat of mine?"

"Here, sir." I handed it to him.

"Whither do you go, sir?" enquired Malone eagerly.

"To do what must be done. Fool that I was, not to see—but 'tis not yet too late." Dr. Johnson lumbered off as the pit began to cry for silence.

We were on pins and needles in our box, but we sat through till Davy Garrick had blessed the land of the Britons and died a noble death, and we joined in the plaudits that rewarded the great actor and the great playwright and the finders of the manuscript. The Ararats were the cynosure of all eyes. It was long till we brought them away from their admirers and down to the church. Percy carried the £100 in a knitted purse. The rain had ceased, and a pale round moon contended with the clouds.

The solemn silence oppressed me as we pushed back the creaking door and entered, and my heart leaped to my mouth when a shadowy figure moved in the silent church. 'Twas Dr. Johnson. He had wrapped himself in his greatcoat, and armed himself with a dark lanthorn. I could smell it, but it showed no gleam.

Without ceremony old Ararat dropped the heavy purse in the empty font and carried young Anthony off for home, promising to return and relieve our watch. I envied Percy and Malone as they, too, departed, with the Red Lion's mulled ale in their minds. They promised to return in an hour's time. Dr. Johnson quenched the lanthorn, and we were left alone in the dark.

I own I liked it little, alone in the dark with the bones of dead men under our feet, and a desperate thief who knows how near? There was no sound. Dead Shakespeare lay under our feet, his effigy stared into the dark above our heads.

We sat in the shadow, back from the font. I fixed my eyes on its pale gleam, whereon the cloudy moon dropped a fitful light through the open door.

I will swear I saw nothing, no shadow on the font, no stealing figure by the open door; I heard nothing, I neither nodded nor closed my eyes. Dr. Johnson fought sleep by my side. The hour was gone, and he was beginning to snore, when the light of a link came toward us, and Percy and Malone came in with the Ararats. Johnson awoke with a snort.

"For this relief much thanks," he muttered. "What, all four of you?"

"Ay," returned Percy, extinguishing the link, "for the Ararats are as eager as we to stand the next watch."

"Let it be so," replied Dr. Johnson, approaching the font, "we will but verify it, that the money is here, and passes from our keeping into yours."

He bent over the font, and his voice changed.

"Pray, gentlemen, step over here."

We did so as he made a light and opened his dark lanthorn.

The money was gone. In its place lay a pile of yellowed papers, thick-writ in a fair court-hand.

Beholding with indescribable feelings this relique of the great English Bard, I fell on my knees and thanked heaven that I had lived to see this day.

"Get up, Bozzy," said Dr. Johnson, "and cease this flummery."

"Oh, sir," I exclaimed, "the very handwriting of the great Bard of Stratford!"

"'Tis not the handwriting of the great Bard of Stratford," retorted Dr. Johnson.

Old Ararat's jaw fell. The boy Anthony opened his mouth and closed it again. By the light of the lanthorn Dr. Percy peered at the topmost page.

"Yet the paper is old," he asserted.

"The paper may be old," replied Dr. Johnson, "yet the words are new."

"Nay, Dr. Johnson," cried old Mr. Ararat, "this is merely to affect singularity. Eminent men from London have certified that my manuscript is genuine, including David Garrick and Dr. Warton."

"Garrick and Warton are deceived," returned Dr. Johnson sternly. "'Caractacus; or, the British Hero' is a modern forgery, and no ancient play."

"Pray, sir, how do you make that good?" enquired Malone.

"I knew it," replied Dr. Johnson, "when I heard King use a word Shakespeare never heard—'mob'—a word shortened from 'mobile' long after Shakespeare died. Nor would Shakespeare have understood the verb 'to compliment'."

"Then," said I, "the thief has had his trouble for his pains, for he has stolen but waste paper indeed."

"Not so," replied Dr. Johnson, "the thief has come nigh to achieving his object, for the thief and the forger are one."

"Name him," cried Dr. Percy. All eyes turned to old Ararat. His face shewed the beginnings of a dumb misery, but no guilt. Anthony's face might have been carved out of a pumpkin.

"If," said Dr. Johnson slowly, "if there were in Stratford a young man, apprenticed to a scrivener and adept with his pen; a young man who has the plays of Shakespeare by heart; and if that young man found as it might be a packet of old paper unused among the dead stationers' gear; is it unreasonable to suppose that that young man was tempted to try out his skill at writing like Shakespeare? And when his skill proved more than adequate, and the play 'Caractacus' was composed and indited, and the Jubilee had raised interest in Shakespeare to fever pitch—what must have been the temptation to put forward the manuscript as genuine?"

"Yet why should he steal his own manuscript?"

"For fear of what has happened," replied Dr. Johnson, "for fear that Dictionary Johnson, the editor of Shakespeare, with his special knowledge might scrutinize the manuscript and detect the imposture."

Old Ararat's face was purple.

"Pray, sir," said Dr. Johnson, "moderate your anger. The boy is a clever boy, and full of promise. Let him be honest from this time forward."

Old Ararat looked at his son, and his jaw worked.

"But, Dr. Johnson," cried Percy, "the hundred pounds!"

Anthony Ararat fell on his knees and raised his hand to Heaven. "I swear before God," he cried vibrantly, "that I never touched the hundred pounds."

It was the first word I had heard out of Anthony. By the fitful light of the lanthorn I stared in amazement at the expressionless face. The boy spoke like a player.

"Believe me, father," cried Anthony earnestly, still on his knees by the font, "I know nothing of the hundred pounds; nor do I know how the manuscript came to be exchanged for the money, for indeed I never meant to restore it until Dr. Johnson was once more far from Stratford."

"He speaks truth," said Dr. Johnson, "for here is the hundred pounds, and it was I who laid the manuscript in the font."

He drew the purse from his capacious pocket and handed it to Dr. Percy.

"How came you by the manuscript?" asked Percy, accepting of the purse.

"It was not far to seek. The forger was the thief. It was likely that the finder was the forger. If Malone's panegyric on my learning frightened him into sequestering the manuscript to prevent it from falling under my eye, then it must have been hid between the time young Anthony left the shop and the time he returned with the empy coffer. He was gone long enough for Mr. Ararat to spin us his long-winded tale. In that space of time he hid the manuscript —surely no further afield than his father's out-buildings. When he came in to us his face and shoulders were wet with rain."

"Tears, surely?"

"Why, his eyes were full of tears. The boy is a comedian. But the drops on his shoulders never fell from his eyes; they were raindrops."

"But, Dr. Johnson," put in Edmond Malone, "we searched the out-buildings thoroughly, and the manuscript was not to be found."

"The manuscript," replied Dr. Johnson, "lay in plain sight before your eyes, and you passed it by without seeing it."

"How could we?" cried Malone, "we turned over the old papers in the shed."

"Did you turn over the other old papers?"

"There were no other old papers."

"There were," said Dr. Percy suddenly, "for when I visited the —the necessary-house, I turned over a pile of old accounts of the greatest interest, put to this infamous use by the carelessness of the householder. I—ah—" his voice trailed off.

"The forged sheets of 'Caractacus' were hastily thrust among them," said Dr. Johnson. "I guessed so much when I heard the allusion to the jakes as the destination of bad poetry. What more likely hiding-place for a day or two, till Dr. Johnson be far from Stratford once more? In short, I left the play and hurried thither, and found the pages undisturbed where young Ararat had thrust them into the heart of the pile."

"Yet if you only meant to sequester the writings, boy," said Dr. Percy sternly, "how came you to offer to barter them for money?"

Anthony rose to his feet.

"Sir," he said respectfully, "I never meant to touch the money. But Dr. Johnson saw clearly, and said so, that 'twas no theft for profit; and I feared that such thoughts might lead him to me. I saw a way by which a thief might profit, and I wrote the letter and dropped it at my father's feet that the deed might seem after all the work of a real thief. Consider my apprehension, sir," he turned to Dr. Johnson, "when you fitted my thumb into the impression it had made."

Dr. Johnson shook his head.

"Too many thumbs fitted it," he said. "Another way must be found to fit a thumb to its print. 'Twas so, too, with the paper. 'Twas clearly from your father's shop; but Percy and I and half Stratford were furnished with the same paper. Again the undistributed middle term."

"Pray, sir, how came you to spare me in your thoughts?" enquired old Ararat.

"I acquitted you," replied Dr. Johnson, "because after Malone's eulogy you never left my side; nor did your thumb fit the print in the wax."

"Pray, Dr. Johnson," added Malone, "coming down here from Mr. Ararat's necessary-house with the manuscript in your pocket, why did you play out the farce? Why not reveal all at once?"

"To amuse Mr. Boswell," replied my friend with a broad smile. "I thought an hour's watch by the bones of Shakespeare, and a dramatic discovery at its end, would give him a rich range of those sensations native to a man of sensibility, and enrich those notes he is constantly taking of my proceedings."

In the laugh that followed at my expense, the Ararats sullenly took themselves off, and we four repaired to the Red Lion.

"Sir," said young Malone, taking leave of us at the door of "Much Ado about Nothing," "this is a lesson in the detection of imposture which I will never forget."

"Sir," said Dr. Johnson, "you are most obliging. Be sure, sir, that I shall stand by you in your every endeavour to make known the truth. Pray, Dr. Percy, accept of the forged manuscript as a memento of the pitfalls of *antiquarianism*."

Dr. Percy accepted with a smile, and we parted on most cordial terms.

"I blush to confess it," I remarked as we prepared to retire, "but I made sure that Dr. Percy was carrying stolen documents about with him in yonder folio-sized packet he was so particular with."

"So he was," remarked Dr. Johnson. "Therefore I exchanged packets with him. I knew with certainty then that Thomas Percy had not stolen the Shakespeare manuscript, for all his antiquarian light fingers."

"How so?" I enquired.

"Because I knew what he *had* stolen."

"What?"

"A household reckoning of the first Anthony Ararat, showing that the good stationer's family consumed an unconscionable quantity of small beer during the year 1614. The magpie clergyman had filched it from old Ararat's necessary-house!"

[Barring larceny, this is the story of William Henry Ireland and his amazing *Vortigern* (1796), transferred to Garrick's Shakespeare Jubilee, which Johnson did not really attend, but Boswell did, blatantly accoutered as described.]

THE TRIPLE-LOCK'D ROOM
(*London, 1775*)

The affair of the triple-lock'd room began as an affair of gallantry, and ended as an affair of mystery and horror. The scene of the tragedy was commonplace enough, being the staymaker's house where I lodged near Piccadilly. The *dramatis personae* all lodged there. The strange knot of Jamaicans had the parlour floor. Sanry the drunken rope-dancer pigged it in the attick. The two-pair-of-stairs floor was divided between James Bruce the Abyssinian traveller and your humble servant, James Boswell younger of Auchinleck, advocate, amateur of crime, and friend to the great Sam: Johnson.

Everybody snubbed the rope-dancer; Bruce the traveller snubbed everybody but the Jamaican lady; and the Jamaican lady snubbed nobody. 'Twas pleasant to attend her levee of mornings before I set out on my daily ramble. On a memorable day in that summer of 1775, Dr. Sam: Johnson was my companion in the lady's chamber.

Her name was Mrs. Winwood. She was newly come to London from the plantations to set up for a lady of fashion, and her *boudoir* lacked no detail of the *ton*. 'Twas all in the Chinese taste. The four-poster bed was richly canopied in China damask. Mr. Chippendale's Chinese chairs were everywhere. There was plenty of red and gold lacquer. An ornate cabinet held ivory knickknacks. Gold dragons two feet high writhed up the japanned coal-box and coiled about its brass handles. The fire-place had a brass fender, and for the summer a fan of white paper in the grate. A Gothick book with gilded margins lay open on a marquetry table, though I seriously doubted whether Mistress Winwood could read its crabbed black-letter. Next it a small Benares coffer, open, revealed a blaze of jewelry within.

We had the field to ourselves, save for the lady's fashionable menagerie of creatures. A motley paraqueet pranced on a carven stand. A snubby creature of the canine kind blinked on a silken cushion, half-closing contemptuous eyes in a sooty face.

"'Tis a picture," cried I, surveying the scene, "from the pencil of Mr. Hogarth!"

"Aye," assented Dr. Johnson, "it shall be called *The Lady's Toilette-table.*"

Indeed only my burly friend himself in his old snuff-brown suit was out of drawing as he sat oscillating upon one of the Chippendale chairs, causing the chair to creak ominously and the Jamaican lady to flinch.

'Twas the sweetest little pink-and-gold pocket Venus ever I saw, sitting at her toilette-table among a confusion of patch-boxes and ribbands, her mask, her fan, her stay-lace, her pomander, lying lost in the litter. She wore a sacque of willow-green tissue, frothing with lace about a bosom more revealed than hid. There were diamonds at throat, wrist, and bosom. The waves of her dusky hair were piled high. She wore a patch like a half-moon beside one liquid black eye, and a patch like a star at the edge of the tiny, perfect pout of her mouth. Her skin glowed like a golden peach. She smiled upon us with pursed lips, making a mouth like a kiss. I could have been her knight-errant.

Much I envied the tiny black page who leaned at her knee. Not that the little savage appreciated his position; for though gorgeous in cloth-of-gold caftan and turban plumed and jewelled, he bore in his ugly brown face a timeless sorrow.

"Sure 'tis a Lilliputian philosopher," remarked Dr. Sam: Johnson, scanning the impassive face.

"A pygmy Nestor—" I concurred.

Johnson quoted:

"Klagge tai ge petontai ep' okeanoio rhoaon,
Andrasi Pygmaioisi phonon kai kera pherousai."

"O, Lord, Sir, spare us your Greek!" cried I. "What does this little animal understand of Homer's works?"

"Little enough, I'll wager. What would you give, my lad," bending to place his great paw on the small cloth-of-gold shoulder, "what would you give to learn about Homer?"

The dark eyes blinked.

"Pompey give what he have, sah," piped the page.

Dr. Johnson was much pleased with his answer.

"Sir," said he to me, "a desire of knowledge is the natural feeling of mankind; and every human being, whose mind is not debauched, will be willing to give all that he has to get knowledge."

I doubt whether either Pompey or his mistress understood this discourse. Dr. Johnson, however, whose good sense keeps pace with his benevolence, omitted to gratify Pompey with an account of the Greek poet. He gratified him rather with a thing more to the purpose, namely sixpence; and the lady, pleased, patted the small golden shoulder.

Standing at her back, her waiting-woman glowered and muttered. Sure never had pocket Venus a stranger Abigail. She was a powerful mulatto, not tall but wide, with watchful black eyes in a broad ugly face. Above her narrow furrowed brow she had twisted a clout of red marked with tortuous figures of black. Her red stuff gown strained with muscles as her arms moved. With an angry jerk she fastened a brilliant pin like a coach-and-four in the lady's tower of curls, and said something between her teeth to the little brown page. He shrank against the lady.

"Ma'am," says Dr. Sam: Johnson bluntly, ignoring this by-play, "you've not brought me hither to discuss Homer. Pray what is it that disquiets you?"

Mistress Winwood gave him a level look.

"I will tell you," said she. "You must know that I went with the company of comedians to Jamaica. I was much admired in both comedy and tragedy, and thus I formed many—friendships—" said the lady delicately, "and received many a gift of jewels, before I married. My husband was a rich planter of Montego Bay, and 'twas his pleasure to adorn me with still handsomer jewels of his own providing. He bought me my mulatto woman, whom you see here, and nothing was wanting that would satisfy me. But alas, within short months, the sultry vapours of Jamaica had carried off my beloved Mr. Winwood, and I was left to mourn."

A tear stole down the golden cheek.

"There was naught left for me but to leave the scene of my sorrow and begin life anew. I realized my holdings. I took my jewels, and Hannah her little son, and hither came we—to find," the comedian inclined gracefully in my direction, "friendship and consolation in Mr. Boswell."

This was fast progress! I returned the inclination, with a smile into which I infused as much meaning as I could.

"What's this to the purpose?" growled Johnson.

"Why, Sir, the jewels. They lie there," she nodded towards the Benares coffer, "and I go in fear for jewels and life together."

"How so, ma'am?"

"Look. I found under my pillow last night—*this*."

Dr. Sam: Johnson looked with contempt on the strange toy she displayed. 'Twas nothing so fearsome, being most like a shuttlecock, made of white feathers bound together with long dark hair. The bunch protruded from a little sack of yellow leather, stuck with seven pins.

"Foh," said Dr. Johnson. "This is a child's toy; this is one of Pompey's amusements. Come here, boy."

Pompey, idly whisking flies by the window, looked around, and began to approach. When he saw the white feather toy he stood stock still, and would approach no further.

"Come on, boy. Acknowledge your property."

Pompey put his little black hands behind him.

"No, sah. Not Pompey's."

He backed into the chimney-corner. As the rusty wig and the glossy black head bent together over the feathered shuttlecock, the jewelled turban sought diversion. First he tried the pug-dog's temper, who shewed ugly teeth. Then he reached up and pulled the paraqueet's tail-feathers. For that he got a sharp jab in his small brown finger, and one crimson drop started. Savagely he bit at the torn place with his sharp white teeth, and his eyes rolled in anger. The next thing I knew, he had bundled the paraqueet, chain and all, into the Chinese box, and slammed the slanting lid. Then ensued such a clanking and squawking as brought the lady from her shuttlecock and the mulatto from the toilette-table. Mistress

Winwood released the indignant bird, which sat on her finger croaking. Hannah gave the erring page a box o' the ear that staggered him, and then dragged him screaming into the backward regions.

As his cries faded, peace returned. Mistress Winwood set the paraqueet back on his perch and refastened the chain. Dr. Johnson returned his attention to the shuttlecock.

"'Twas under my pillow," the lady told him, "and I found it there in the morning. And last night after I blew out my candle, something outside tried to lift the hook on my door. I cried out, and it went away."

"Let us look at this door-fastening." Dr. Sam: Johnson heaved his great bulk erect and lumbered to the door. The lady followed him, and I followed her.

'Twas the slightest of hooks, that fell into a loop of metal affixed to the jamb.

"'Twill never do, ma'am," says my ingenious friend. "Any knife-blade can lift it from without. We'll fix you bolts above and below, that shall repel intruders and make you and your jewels safe."

"Let it be as you wish," said the lady. "Yet I trust no lock nor bolt, I. Pray, Mr. Boswell, take upon you to watch my door from without, that nobody enters to do me harm."

The lady put forth this unreasonable request with so ravishing a smile, I had no heart to refuse; though in truth I had preferred to be a watcher 'tother side of the bolt.

"Then I'll join you," cried Dr. Johnson, reading my mind, "to preserve the proprieties."

"Damn your proprieties!" cried I inwardly.

As we stood thus clustered about the door, a mighty rapping upon the other side of the panel startled us. We gave ground.

"Enter," said Mistress Winwood.

Whereupon, ducking under the door-frame, in marched quite the tallest man I had ever seen without first paying a fee. 'Twas James Bruce, the Abyssinian traveller, who lodged in the second floor front. He stood a magnificent seven feet.

'Twas my first view of my fellow-lodger. Mistress Winwood made him known to us, and he bowed without a word. His presence in the lady's chamber, seven feet tall and handsome as a god, boded little good to the suit of James Boswell, five feet odd and indifferent pretty. I seated myself sullenly.

The seven-foot Scotchman chose a dubious Chippendale chair, and sat mum. We sat as mum, and tried to freeze him. But the lady shone upon him. Under her smile and her wide-eyed interest, he thawed indeed, and began to regale us with wonders. I saw Dr. Sam: Johnson shift and mutter uneasily at the romantick traveller's story. We must needs hear of the fabled lyre of the antient Egyptians–

"There's one liar the less in Egypt," muttered Dr. Johnson *sotto voce*, "now that you're returned to London–"

Unhearing, the fabulous traveller fabled on, of the Abyssinians, who cut their steaks from the living cow, and the Watussi, a race of giants, who absolutely looked down their noses at a mere seven feet, and the Wambutti–

"Who," burst in Johnson, unable to brook more wonders, "have no doubt their heads beneath their shoulders, as Mandeville fabled before you. Sir, your servant, I've had enough of romantick extravagance, so I'll e'en take my leave. Ma'am, yours, and we'll wait upon you after supper."

Perforce I made my bow, and left the giant master of the field.

As we mounted to my lodging above, we encountered the rope-dancer. He was running, absolutely running, down the balustrade. The man had the feet of a fly. When he saw me, he came to a halt by dropping lightly to the landing. He seized me by the lappet and breathed alcoholic fumes in my face.

"Pray, Mr. Boswell," he whined, "a trifle till Monday; for then I'll be *flush* of the *cole*, I assure 'ee, 'tis Hoxham Fair, and I'll dance on the rope again."

I looked at the narrow keel of a face, the rough wigless head, the closeset darting eyes, and liked him ill.

"Be off," said I, "for I've nothing on me."

"Then I know who has," replied he insolently, "where there's a little fellow-feeling too for a poor mountebank–"

And he danced off down the stair on his long shoeless toes. I heard him clatter at the Jamaican actress's door. So, Mr. Abyssinian traveller, I reflected sourly, where's your tête-à-tête now?

'Twas the rope-dancer, after all, who held the field. He was still there when we returned after supper, wigless and unbuttoned, working his long unshod feet on the fender and drinking tea from a flowery saucer. He pulled a long face when he saw us, and rose unwillingly to go. As he strolled to the door he jingled a pocketful, as if to flaunt the success of his errand. At the door he turned with his hand on the latch. He gave the Jamaican lady a servile congee, included us in an insolent nod, and drew the door softly to.

"Poor man," said Mistress Winwood, "the life of the stroller is thorny."

We in our turn drank tea from flowery saucers. Then we gave the lady into the broad black hands of Hannah, who dighted her for bed while we waited in the passage.

When the pug and the paraqueet had been turned out, and the black woman had retired to her pallet, it came our turn. Quietly we entered the chamber. How my heart beat as the tinkling voice greeted us from the shadow of the Chinese damask bed-curtains. The lady lay on the pillow, pallid as her linens, in a cloud of black hair. Her night-rail was another froth of lace, held with a diamond brooch.

"Have no fear, ma'am," says Dr. Sam: Johnson, "for here's what shall make all secure."

From his capacious pocket he dragged two stout bolts, and we proceeded to affix them on either side the hook, half-way up and half-way down the stout wooden door.

"Now, ma'am," says he, "with your permission I'll e'en make fast the window—"

"There's no need," says she, "for the wall falls sheer."

"Here's a balcony," said Dr. Johnson, peering out into the summer moonlight.

"That only a fly could come at," replied Mistress Winwood, "on that smooth brick wall."

"Then we'll lock out the flies," said Dr. Johnson firmly, and swung the catch tight.

"And pray, Dr. Johnson," whispered the lady, shame-faced, "look under the bed."

We looked under the bed. No desperado lurked there. But Dr. Johnson advanced the candle, and from a murky corner picked up some small object. On our knees on the Chinese rug we scanned it. 'Twas another shuttlecock. Dr. Johnson shook his head over it, and hastily concealed it from the lady in his capacious pocket.

"Nothing," said he to Mistress Winwood; "but we'll give the rest of the chamber a turnout."

We looked in the wardrobe. Nothing but the lady's silken gowns, breathing otto. We looked up the chimney. Nothing but soot. We looked into every corner that might conceal a man. Nothing but candle-shadows.

"All's safe, ma'am," said Dr. Johnson. "Do you hook and bolt after us, and your citadel is triple-lock'd."

"Good night," whispered she.

I bowed in the dark, not daring to approach and kiss her hand, and we took our leave.

Behind us we heard the hook fall into place and the bolts ram home.

There was a damask sofa in the shadowy hall, and there we sat ourselves. The line of light under the door died as the lady blew out her candle. The house was still a while.

Beside me Dr. Sam: Johnson yawned mightily.

"This is a sleeveless errand," muttered he. "We have eased the lady's mind; let us ease ourselves with a bed. Nothing can come at Mistress Winwood through yonder triple-lock'd door. Come, let us go up."

'Twas my secret hope that through the triple-lock'd door, if I but waited long enough, would come the lady seeking the solace of my presence,

"Do you go up," said I.

"You'll come with me," said my stern mentor, "for a rake-helly young dog."

I could but laugh, and follow. We stole to the house-door, and opened it gently. I thought at the far end of the passage a door was eased open, but I could not be sure. We drew the door to, and mounted the stair.

My coat and waistcoat were off, and I was attacking my breeches-buttons, when I heard Mistress Winwood scream. In my shirt as I was I ran down the stair, and Dr. Sam: Johnson lumbered behind. As I ran the screaming ceased abruptly, to be succeeded by a silence more sinister yet. I ran down the long hall, thrust aside the mulatto woman where she stood dumbly shaking the door-handle, and flung myself against the panels.

We had done our work too well. The three locks held. Dr. Johnson added his great strength to mine, but to no purpose. If one lock gave, the others held it in line.

In a moment the seven-foot Scotchman ran in in his shirt-sleeves. In another moment the shoeless rope-dancer joined us, fully sober and fully cloathed, with his hair on end. We all four rushed at the door. It was too stout.

"Fetch the axe!" cried Dr. Johnson.

"Fetch a rope!" cried the mountebank. "If a rope be stretched from yonder tree opposite my window, I'll engage to walk across and so in at Mistress Windwood's casement."

"'Tis lock'd."

"A window may be smashed."

"A door may be smashed. Fetch the axe."

"Do you wield the axe. I'll adventure by the rope."

"Do so," cried the Abyssinian traveller. "I've what shall assist you, which I used in climbing the Mountains of the Moon. 'Tis as it were a grappling hook, which shall carry your rope from the ground to the balcony, and so a man may swarm up like a monkey."

"Do you break in like a monkey," cried Dr. Sam: Johnson contemptuously, "I'll break in like a man. Where's the axe?"

The explorer and the rope-dancer rushed off. The mulatto was dispatched backwards for the axe. We once more put our shoulders to the stout panels. In vain. At last we desisted and wiped our brows.

At that instant we heard from within the tinkle of breaking glass, and then the window creaked up. Another long moment, and we heard the three locks released. The door opened, and the mountebank stood before us. He was whiter than his ruffles.

"Mistress Winwood is dead," said he.

We stepped sombrely in. The mountebank touched flame to the candles. James Bruce hauled himself over the sill and entered; his shoes crunched on the broken glass of the window.

The Jamaican lady lay dead in her bed. A carving knife was buried to the hilt in the disordered laces of her night-rail. Save for that disorder, the room was as we left it.

"This is the work of the devil himself!" cried the mountebank, going green as he took in the situation. He looked fearfully behind him at our shadows wavering on the wall. "The window was lock'd tight; I had to break it. The door was hooked and double-bolted; you heard me lift the hook and undo the twin bolts. How could anything human do this, and make its way out again?"

A horrible cry, as from the Tartarian Lake, broke out behind us. With jangled nerves I forced my head to turn. The mulatto stood in the doorway with the axe in her hand. As I looked at her she dropped the axe and fell to the floor by the bedside.

"Damballa Oueddo!" she cried. "Ezilee! Ogoun Badagris!"

"These are devils she calls on!" cried the rope-dancer. "This woman it is that has called up fiends to do this devil's work!"

"This is devil's work," said Dr. Johnson heavily, "and the devil is flown through the triple-lock'd door; or it is man's work—and the man is still here."

With one consent we fell to searching. The mulatto woman ignored us, and pursued her own strange rites. She cut a tress of the shadowy hair, and bound it around her wrist. She traced on the floor, in powder, designs I could not fathom. When the designs were complete, and muttered over, she set about kindling a fire. Dr. Johnson did not check her; he had already got soot on his venerable brow assuring himself there was still nothing else up the chimney. Backward she went for coals. I stared at her strength; she heaved the hod in, filled, as easily as she had carried it out. It must have held a quarter-chaldron.

Hunched over the grate she struck flint and steel. The paper fan blazed; she blew up the coals. When she had a good glow, she laid aside the bellows and, crouching over the flame, she began to mutter. Again she called upon Damballa and Ogoun Badagris, rocking herself from side to side.

Our search was over. We had repeated in every detail our search of one short hour before; and as before, had found nothing. We stood to watch the woman's curious proceedings.

"What do you do, good woman?" enquired Bruce curiously.

"I find the murderer. I see him in the flame."

"This is a rank superstition!" cried Dr. Johnson.

"Sir," said Bruce, "it may be; but I have seen in Africa such things as have made me wonder. What do you see, good woman?"

"I see a man. He comes down like a juju from the sky. He breaks the window, and turns back the bolt, and enters the room. I see him approach my lady. She screams. He strikes. Ah!"

The woman hid her face and wailed. The rope-dancer turned to Bruce.

"Your balcony is directly above. How easy to descend—"

"And break the glass?" Bruce caught him up. "*You* broke the glass. I saw you do it."

"And we heard you!" cried I.

"Perhaps Mistress Winwood admitted him," said the rope-dancer.

"If you were a gentleman," I cried hotly, "I'd call you to account for such a word!"

"Nay," said Bruce coolly, "let him prate. If the lady let me in, who let me out after the lady lay dead? Who shot the bolts after me? Robin Goodfellow belike? Or was it done by enchantment?"

"Why," said I slowly, "there's a way to shoot bolts from without. 'Tis done with packthread, and they shewed in court how it was done when they tried Sarah Malcolm."

"And the hook?"

"There must be a way for that too."

"And so," said Bruce with his cold smile, "you came running, and found me at the door with a handful of packthread!"

"We did not, Sir," owned Dr. Johnson. "Enough of this. This is matter for Bow Street. Let the watch be called."

I bellowed "Pompey!" into the hall. The rope-dancer at the broken window was bawling "Watch!"

"The child is too little," protested Hannah. "He will get lost."

The child in question came trotting down the hall to cut her short. He was in his little shirt-tail, rubbing his eyes as he trotted along.

"Pompey here, sah."

A shout from the rope-dancer ended the matter. The watch had heard, and was even now upon the stair. Another moment, and in came the watchman in his antient coat to the heels, with his flapped hat, his lanthorn, and his staff. He saw at once how things stood, and acted decisively. First he opened the coffer of jewels.

"They are all there," said Hannah. "Nothing is missing."

Then he bellowed for his mate, and they took us all up.

They took us up!—me, James Boswell Esq: of Auchinleck, James Bruce the Abyssinian traveller, and Dr. Sam: Johnson the great lexicographer!

I would have made indignant proclamation of our names and qualities, but Dr. Johnson checked me with a look. The great man preferred to spend the night in the round-house with an unemployed rope-dancer and two Jamaican slaves!

So to the round-house we went. As we paraded on the pavement, I saw in the moonlight the rope dangling from the balcony, by which the rope-dancer had ascended. The great grappling-hook was plain to see, caught over the balcony rail. It had three prongs, and a ball to throw it by.

Late ramblers must have stared at the strange procession. As was his unhappy wont, Dr. Sam: Johnson lurched along muttering to himself, and touching the posts of the footway as he passed. The rope-dancer's narrow feet skimmed along without shoes; he seemed oblivious of the uneven paving-blocks. The mulatto woman slouched and mumbled. James Bruce the Abyssinian traveller strode along like a king. At first little Pompey trotted along behind like a puppy; but after a while Mr. Bruce took pity on his short legs and hoisted him to a towering shoulder.

Thus, each wrapped in who knows what thoughts, our ill-assorted company came to the round-house, and passed within. 'Twas an unfriendly structure of old brick and stone. I cannot say what amenities were provided in the forward chamber for the refreshing of the watch. We were thrust into the detention hold. A stale smell insulted our nostrils. Stark stone was rough under foot; the walls were bare. A rough deal table held the center; long benches lined the walls. Narrow windows interposed bars between us and the moonlight. Sixpence to the watch brought us an exiguous farthing dip, which did little to dispel the gloom of the place. As if from far away came the rumble of coach-wheels and the cries of roysterers between taverns.

'Twas an uneasy place to spend the night, most like some antient tower in the wastes of Africa. As if it had been so, Abyssinian Bruce laid himself stoically down like an old campaigner. The rope-dancer paced like a tiger on his noiseless unshod feet. The mulatto woman sat and stared; her Lilliputian philosopher curled himself up like a dog in the corner. 'Twas our luck that we had the place to ourselves. I stared up at the full moon through the barred window.

"Unravel me this, Sir," said I to my learned friend, seated bolt upright on the bench. "If 'twas not the devil, who was it?"

"One of these," he replied softly. "One of these. Watch."

"Watch for what?"

"Let 'em smoulder, they'll smoak themselves," said he.

The staymaker's lodgers smouldered as the moon swung over the sky. The rope-dancer kept up his noiseless pacing. Hannah sat rigid, and muttered. Curled in his corner Pompey slept the sleep of childhood, and stretched on the bench the imperturbable explorer slept like a child too. My friend and I waked, and heard nothing. The moon was waning as Dr. Johnson leaned towards me and said in a loud whisper:

"'Tis taedious to wait, but soon now we'll have this murderer."

"How so?"

"Why, I can tell you how," boomed my friend with unnecessary loudness. "You must know, this knifehandle was of an exotick wood, which stains the hand. The stain deepens as time passes. This murderer will be caught, my friend, *red-handed.*"

The rope-dancer resumed his steady pacing. Hannah swayed and muttered. Silence thickened.

A moment later my friend nudged me sharply, and I followed

his gaze. Outlined against the narrow window was the mulatto woman. By the uncertain light of the moon she was staring intently at the palms of her hands.

"Never fear," said Dr. Johnson to me in his bull's mutter, "we'll be cleared before the face of the magistrate. Trust me, this murderer cannot escape. There's a diamond missing, d'ye see; I missed it from the lady's night-rail though Hannah did not. The murderer carries it on his person; and when he's searched, 'tis all up with him."

The rope-dancer stopped his pacing, and stood stock still. The mulatto woman stiffened. The Abyssinian traveller lay like the dead. Then the mulatto woman began to mutter between her teeth, angrily, without stopping. Pompey in his corner slept unstirring. Suddenly the woman's wrath fell upon the hapless page. She hauled him out from under the bench, and addressed her biting patois to him. The little page answered placatingly, but the woman was not to be placated. Words brought blows; she shook him till his teeth rattled, and then blows rained about his shoulders, till Dr. Johnson was fain to step between them.

"Nay, ma'am, enough," said he, shielding the hapless victim.

The woman gave over, and Pompey crept sobbing away from her under the bench. Gradually his sobs died away, and once more silence fell.

The rope-dancer tired of his pacing. Clutching his wild elf-locks in both hands, he sank to the bench beside Bruce. The traveller breathed heavily, and the rope-dancer bent over him, feeling his heart, before resuming his pacing. Suddenly Dr. Johnson spoke aloud.

"Mr. Bruce! Oblige me by handing me the diamond brooch which is in your left-hand waistcoat pocket."

Bruce came out of sleep standing up.

"I have taken no diamond brooch."

"Pray, Sir, don't quibble. The brooch is in your left-hand waistcoat pocket."

Bruce put up his heavy brows, and turned out the pocket. There was a flash of light in the moon as the diamond brooch fell to the stone floor.

"Sir," said Bruce steadily, "I give you my word of honour as a gentleman, I neither stabbed this unfortunate lady, nor stole her diamond brooch, which I now see for the first time."

"I believe you," cried I, "for 'tis clear this rope-dancer *planted* it on you, 'tis he that stabbed the lady for her jewels."

"Never believe it," said Bruce; "how did the poor man enter that triple-lock'd room and leave all lock'd again behind him?"

"Somebody did," said I, "that's plain to a demonstration."

"Why," says Dr. Johnson, "the rope-dancer did; he broke the window and turned the latch and so entered."

"I'll confess," cried the wretched rope-dancer. "I did indeed take the brooch—the lady was dead, she needed it no more, and my need was sore—but as God sees me, I never laid a finger on her, for she was good to me in my need."

He sank to the bench, and sobbed.

For a space there was no noise but his heavy gasping. Bruce composed himself again to slumber. The mulatto woman sat in sullen silence. Once the door creaked on its hinges, and we thought the watch had come for us; but nothing appeared at the crack, and the door creaked to again.

Suddenly from without there was an outcry. The heavy shouting of the watch and their thudding footsteps changed in the sound of blows and screams of pain. Then the door jerked open, and the watchman shoved a small figure through the door in a heap. 'Twas Pompey. We had not seen his evasion, for he had slipped through noiselessly on his belly, most like some little reptile. He returned sobbing and cringing, and holding his head, which rang with the watchmen's blows.

My merciful friend picked up the small shaking form, and set him on his knee.

"Never cry, Pompey," said he.

"She beat me," sobbed Pompey.

"Never mind," said Dr. Sam: Johnson slowly; his long shapely fingers gently stroked the small brown cheek.

"And they beat me," added Pompey, and wept afresh.

"Be comforted," said Dr. Johnson. "Do thou stay by me, I'll tell thee a story. I'll tell thee of—"

He seemed to cast about for some suitable narrative. Memory suggested his choice.

"I'll tell thee of Homer, as I promised," said he, and repeated some lines in Greek; the round-house rang with his sonorous voice.

I thought the little savage ever less likely to be entertained with Greek.

"Which is to say," said Dr. Johnson, "in the words of Alexander Pope:

"With shouts the Trojans, rushing from afar,
Proclaim their motions, and provoke the war:
So when inclement winters vex the plain
With piercing frosts, or thick-descending rain,
To warmer seas the cranes embodied fly,
With noise, and order, through the midway sky;
To pygmy nations wounds and death they bring,
And all the war descends upon the wing.

"But you are not to suppose," Dr. Johnson instructed his unlikely pupil, "that these bird-contests ever happened, for 'tis only a fable."

"Nay, Sir," struck in the Abyssinian traveller, "there you are out, for in Africa—"

"Tut, Sir, a crane's but a bird, even in Africa."

"In Africa, Sir—"

The door was pushed roughly open, and the watch were there.

"You must come along to Bow Street," said the leader.

"Not I," said Dr. Sam: Johnson, "but you may take the murderer."

His powerful arms clamped like a vise upon the tiny figure in his lap.

The metamorphosis was astounding. One moment the small figure was nestled trustingly and innocently against the great shoulder. The next, it was a small fury, writhing, scratching, and biting, and cursing steadily in a strong new voice, in patois, African, and surprisingly good English. Then the mulatto woman struck like a fury, and we had all we could do to hold her off.

"Do you mean to tell me," I demanded incredulously, "that that small child stabbed his mistress?"

We sat at breakfast at the Mitre Tavern. Hannah and Pompey had been committed to Newgate, and now 'twas time to refresh ourselves after the fatigues of the night. Sombre James Bruce ate sparingly of bread and cheese; the hungry rope-dancer stuffed himself with buttock of beef; Dr. Johnson called for a cut of cold veal pye, and ate with relish.

"'Tis no small child," said Dr. Johnson, "but a grown man, a very dangerous desperado cast in Lilliputian mould."

Boswell: "Yet his mother—"

Johnson: "Foh, Hannah is not his mother."

"Of that you may be sure," said Abyssinian Bruce, "for they are of different races."

Johnson: "Hannah is his accomplice; and in all probability his mistress, for there is no human freak so freakish but he may find a woman to love him. They have confessed it, 'twas a deep-laid plot to come to England and be free; for 'tis known among the slaves, since the case of Sommersett three years since, that the slave is free the moment he sets foot on the free soil of England. So the new-bought slave-woman palms off her paramour as her child, and Mistress Winwood brings them hither. Now they will tarry with her only so long as will serve to prepare a refuge, and then steal the jewels and make off. Vigilance detected the first attempt—"

Boswell: "What part did the shuttlecock play?"

Bruce: "'Twas a sleepy charm; I have seen such things in my travels."

Johnson snapped his finger at the dawdling waiter, and more veal pye came on the run.

"So, Sir," said he, loading a mouthful, "a new plot was necessitated. Being unable to enter from without, Hannah bethought herself to hide her tiny accomplice in the lock'd room—"

Boswell: "Where: We searched the place."

Johnson: "We searched for a man. Had we been searching for a child, we would have looked in the coal-box, and found him."

Boswell: "What a risque!"

Johnson: "No risque at all, though he were caught there—simply another childish prank. He played his part well."
Boswell: "'Twas a mad risque to make the attempt the very night we were to watch."
Johnson: "They did not know of it. The plan was concerted, by chance, in their absence, and carried out after the woman was withdrawn. Concealed in the coal-box, Pompey heard us affix the bolts; but he doubted not he could draw them easily enough, and so make off. The bolted-door mystification was no part of his scheam."
Boswell: "Yet what folly, to set so weak an arm to assassination."
Johnson: "'Tis not so weak an arm, as I found when I tried to hold him. Nor was assassination intended; he was but to snatch the gems, and make off. But Mistress Winwood waked and screamed, and in panick he silenced her. He had no time to unlock the triple locks; he must hide again. Then indeed was he in danger, had he been discovered; but he could do no other. Soon enough his accomplice's wit taught her how to carry the coal-box out of danger without being suspected."
Boswell (*thoughtfully*): "I made sure that the rope-dancer had done it by trickery. Say the scream was counterfeited, the lady but drugged within. Then the man who enters her smashed window in sight of witnesses may privily stab her before he opens the door and admits—"

The rope-dancer threw down the great bone he was gnawing, leaped to his shoeless feet, and hauled me up by the cravat.

"Ha' done," he cried roughly, "or gentleman or no you'll fight me."

James Bruce pulled him down on the bench with one great hand.

"With me so close on your heels," said he calmly, "Dr. Johnson knew better. Pray, Dr. Johnson, how did you smoak Pompey's imposture?"

"Well, Sir," replied Dr. Johnson as I settled my ruffles and the rope-dancer glowered upon his bone, "as we sat in the round-house, I tried one trick and another to learn the truth. I put forth the fable of the knife that stains the hand; and Hannah must needs examine her hands. Then she had been handling the knife. 'Twas no fable that a gem was missing. When I said so, it brought confusion, for there was guilt in two hearts. Our friend here thought to get clear of the gem, thrust in his matted poll; I was watching, and I saw the attempt. Hannah thought her accomplice was seeking to cheat her of part of the swag, and swinged him soundly for it. When Hannah turned against him, Pompey thought best to take to his heels before anger brought betrayal. And 'twas thus he betrayed himself."

"How so?"

"I took pity on a beaten child, took him on my knee, and patted his cheek. There is no mistaking a man's cheek that has gone a day without the razor. At first my mind could scarce believe what my fingers told me. But I began to recollect what historians tell us, how Augustus had his dwarf, and Constantine had one no bigger than a partridge; Mark Antony had one under two feet in height, and Domitian assembled them by troops; Catherine de Medici bred the little creatures. Why not then a waiting dwarf in Mistress Winwood's household?"

"What erudition, Sir!" cried Bruce.

"Aye," said I slyly, "on the part of *The Universal Magazine*, whence all these antient instances come."

"'Twas then clear," went on Johnson, ignoring me with grandeur, "whose arm had the nerve for the deed, and whose frame was small enough to hide safely in a room we searched. I held him amused till the watch came; I assure you 'twas a strange experience, reciting Homer while I held a dangerous murderer on my knee."

"'Twas an interposition of Providence," said the rope-dancer.

"Which found a learned instrument," said Abyssinian Bruce, bowing to my ingenious friend. "Yet in one thing, Dr. Johnson, you are out. Pompey is no freak of nature, but a member of the race of pygmies that inhabit the African forest. Whether they battle the cranes, I will not say; but had you listened, instead of shouting me down, you would have heard what report speaks of the race of the Wambutti, the African pygmy, a race stunted, but clever, adroit, and strong. Now, Sir, the Wambutti—"

"You, Sir," cried Dr. Johnson, cutting the discourse short, "may have heard travellers' tales of the pygmies; but *I*, Sir, (swelling) *I* am the man who caught one alive."

[This bit of fiction began with such a blackamoor page as Hogarth drew in *Marriage à la Mode*, accreting the fictitious Jamaicans and the real African Traveller as it developed.]

ABOUT THE AUTHOR

Lillian de la Torre was born in New York on March 15, 1902, and christened Lillian de la Torre Bueno (subsequently shortening the name to provide her pseudonym). She was brought up in a house full of books, including a rich collection of early detective stories, which marked her for life. In graduate school her field of special interest was the Age of Johnson, soon to provide both the inspiration and the materials for her continuing short story series about Dr. Sam: Johnson, detector.

As the wife of George S. McCue of Colorado College (now retired), Miss de la Torre has spent almost fifty productive years in Colorado Springs, Colorado.

Half of her twelve published books are in her chosen field of historical mystery and crime, including *Elizabeth Is Missing, The Heir of Douglas, The Truth about Belle Gunness,* and a play, *Goodbye, Miss Lizzie Borden.* Two biographies for teens, an anthology, and two cook books (co-authored), and a collection of verse, with numerous articles both "learned" and otherwise, complete the list.

Her hobbies are amateur theatre as actress and playwright, choral singing, travel for pleasure as well as research; and cooking, a daily adventure.

Still active, Miss de la Torre is now working on the mystery of the "Kidnapped Earl," and her "Dr. Sam: Johnson, detector" short stories continue to appear now and then in *Ellery Queen's Mystery Magazine.*